BAD HAIR DAY

ALSO BY CARRIE HARRIS

BAD
TASTE
in BOYS

BAD HAIR DAY

CARRIE HARRIS

DELACORTE PRESS

Text copyright © 2012 by Carrie Harris
Jacket photograph copyright © 2012 by Ashley Lebedev/Trevillion Images

All rights reserved. Published in the United States by Delacorte Press, an imprint of Random House Children's Books, a division of Random House, Inc., New York.

Delacorte Press is a registered trademark and the colophon is a trademark of Random House, Inc.

randomhouse.com/teens

Educators and librarians, for a variety of teaching tools, visit us at RHTeachersLibrarians.com

Library of Congress Cataloging-in-Publication Data
Harris, Carrie.
Bad hair day / Carrie Harris. — 1st ed.
p. cm.
Summary: Future physician Kate Grable is thrilled to shadow the county medical examiner, but when he is arrested for murder and Kate is left to run the morgue, she discovers that something is killing students—something very hairy and strong.
ISBN 978-0-385-74215-3 (hardcover)—ISBN 978-0-375-99044-1 (glb)—
ISBN 978-0-307-97419-8 (ebook)
[1. Werewolves—Fiction. 2. Murder—Fiction. 3. Forensic sciences—Fiction. 4. High schools—Fiction. 5. Schools—Fiction. 6. Horror stories.] I. Title.
PZ7.H241228Bab 2012
[Fic]—dc23
2011037078

The text of this book is set in 14-point Seria.

Book design by Heather Daugherty

Printed in the United States of America
10 9 8 7 6 5 4 3 2 1
First Edition

TO CONNOR, LILY, AND RENEE.
YOU (AND YOUR HAIR) INSPIRE ME.

ACKNOWLEDGMENTS

Most days, I can't believe my luck. So when I sat down to write these acknowledgments, the first thing that came to mind was something along the lines of "THANK YOU TO EVERYBODY I'VE EVER MET! EEEEEEEEEEEEEEEEEE!" Only in my head, it's skywritten in sparkly bubble letters. Because everyone knows sparkles make everything better.

But there are some people in particular I really do need to thank. My family: Andy, Connor, Lily, and Renee. Very few people would put up with my requests to jump off trains with me, or chop watermelons with katanas, or put sugar on your lips and mug for the camera. I think it's pretty awesome to be part of a family where "weird" is the highest compliment. You make me so deliriously happy. Thank you for making me excited to wake up every day, even if I'm grumpy at first!

My writing partners—Kiki Hamilton, Keri Mikulski, Ellen Oh, Laura Riken, Kiersten White, and Natalie Whipple—are made of the sauce of awesome. And I owe a special debt of gratitude to the members of Class of 2k11 for being my lifeboat in 2011.

Kate Schafer Testerman and Wendy Loggia, you two are rock stars! I feel so honored to know you, let alone work with you. And the rest of the crew at Delacorte Press? You are crazy geniuses, plain and simple.

A special shout-out goes to the shambling hordes online who send my silly videos, tweet with me about stuff that makes me wonder about our collective sanity, and zombify themselves to give me a laugh. Honestly? Hearing from you is one of the best parts of this whole author gig.

CHAPTER one

"**B**raaaaains!"

After all the zombie attacks, even the word made me twitchy. Especially when repeatedly moaned by an annoying freshman in the school bus loop at eight a.m. As if I wasn't annoyed enough already—I'd gotten to school early because the Future Doctors of America program started today. According to plan, we should have been bouncing across the railroad tracks on Washington Ave. right about now. But instead, I stood in the gray winter slush with my fellow FDA students, watching the underclassmen arrive for school and scanning the loop in vain for the bus. It was fourteen and a half minutes late. The program would be starting without me; watching people act like complete morons only added insult to injury.

The freshman elbowed his buddies before putting his backpack on his head and staggering around with his arms outstretched. They laughed so hard I thought they'd burst something. Some people thought the zombie virus was hilarious. Obviously, they hadn't seen the victims; my boyfriend's best friend was still in assisted living. Brain damage. So I didn't think it was all that funny when zombie boy staggered over and accidentally grabbed my breasts, one in each hand. And when I say accidentally, I really mean on purpose.

I knocked his hands off my chest, grabbed him by one backpack strap, and yanked him close enough to talk right in his ear. Or right in his backpack, anyway.

"Listen up, dork," I said in the most pleasant voice possible, which wasn't very pleasant at all. "I don't have the time or the masochistic tendencies necessary to deal with you. So how about you keep out of my way, and I'll pay you the same courtesy?"

He dumped the backpack on the ground and pushed me off. For a moment, I thought maybe he'd back down, but then his so-called friends started in on him.

"Uh-oh, Damian. I think you pissed her off!" crowed one.

"Look out! She's gonna stake you!" added another.

"That's for vampires, you morons," I muttered, turning away. Not my smartest move. Damian-the-freshman didn't like being taunted, so he shoved me to save face. It didn't hurt or anything; I'm tougher than I look. But my backpack spilled all over the ground, and that ticked me off.

I'd never hit anybody before, but this was really the last straw. He was lucky someone interceded before I could swing.

"Hey, calm down."

Trey Black stepped in front of me. He was a recent transfer from Southern California. Why anyone would want to trade that kind of weather for Ohio winters was beyond me. But here he was, and apparently he'd designated himself the sworn protector of freshman idiocy. I needed to get him together with my brother, Jonah. Jonah was the poster child for freshman idiocy.

I let out a long breath in a vain attempt to calm myself as I bent down to pick up my stuff. Trey had this knack for making me uncomfortable. He had tousled blond hair and surfer-boy good looks, and I wasn't totally immune to that. But I had a boyfriend, and they were friends, so it felt really wrong when he acted flirty. Or looked at me. Or stood within fifteen feet of me. The fact that he flirted with anything in a skirt didn't make it any easier to deal with.

"You okay?" He bent down beside me to pluck my calculus book from a mound of dirt-speckled snow. "You look pretty upset."

"Yeah." I glared at Damian, who flipped me off before heading to class with his friends. "Just a little stressed."

"What's wrong?"

He handed me the book with one of his patented charming smiles, his fingers grazing mine. A girl getting off the bus across from us took one look at him and nearly fainted. I tried to act like the "accidental" caress was no big deal, but I could feel the embarrassed heat in my cheeks. I started stuffing the books into my backpack. The worst part about it all was that he had never crossed the line, so I couldn't be sure if I was overreacting.

"Just crazy busy this week," I babbled. "I was up until almost midnight working on my slave-trade paper for American history, and I've got a huge pile of FDA makeup work, and I'm still not done with all the Rockathon prep, and my mom's coming back from Germany this week. After it's all over, I think I might go into hibernation."

"Well, if you need any help . . ." He sidled closer to me. There was no way for me to stand up without getting within kissing distance. My legs started shaking from being crouched over too long, but the only choices were standing and giving Trey the wrong impression or plopping butt-first into half-melted bus slop.

I would have been stuck there forever if Aaron hadn't walked over. But the minute he did, Trey backed off. Aaron Kingsman—my boyfriend—was smart, sweet, and salivatingly gorgeous, not that I was biased or anything. He was also the quarterback of our football team. I tried not to hold that against him. In return, he tried to pretend I wasn't a semi-reformed nerd. I couldn't decide which one of us had the more difficult task.

Trey's face broke out into a huge grin. Seriously, he adored my boyfriend more than I did. I kept expecting him to tattoo Aaron in a big heart on his arm, but it hadn't happened yet. Maybe he had put it on his butt instead.

"Hey, bro." He punched Aaron on the shoulder. "Haven't seen you in the weight room lately. Where've you been?"

"Sorry, just busy," Aaron replied. He didn't brush Trey off, exactly, but he pulled me to my feet and wrapped me in a hug. "Everything okay, Kate?"

I couldn't complain, not with everything Aaron was going through. He went to visit his friend Mike every week, but the brain damage was so bad that Mike couldn't remember who Aaron was. And part of that was my fault because I'd unknowingly helped my crazy teacher develop the zombie virus. But I'd cured it too; that had to count for something. So I pushed away my problems and said, "Yeah. Trey helped rescue me from a wannabe zombie."

Aaron snorted. "You don't need anyone to rescue you from anything, Kate."

"Exactly." Trey looked me up and down behind Aaron's back.

Luckily, I didn't have to reply. The bus pulled into the loop and screeched to a stop. When the door hissed open, Mrs. Gilbert, the FDA program liaison, stuck her head out with a slightly panicked smile. I would have been worried except that slight panic was her default setting. I could relate to that.

"All right, everyone!" she said. "We're running a bit late here, so I'd appreciate it if you'd move move move!"

She clapped to punctuate each move. Either she was on drugs or she spent way too much time watching television shows meant for preschoolers. Or both.

All I wanted to do was get on the bus, but I only made it two steps before Aaron grabbed me by the shoulders. I expected a kiss, but he spun me around instead. Then he opened my backpack. I was just about to ask him what the heck he was doing when he handed me an antibac wipe. My savior.

"You sure you're okay?" he said, his breath warm against my ear. "Your hands are all dirty, and you look like you swallowed a lemon."

"I'm just tense today. And some moron dumped my books." I scrubbed the grime off my fingers and leaned back against him. I could hear the steady beat of his heart. It was the kind of thing I could have listened to forever, although I would have died before I admitted that out loud.

"You know I trust you to take care of yourself, but I'd really love to beat him up for you. Could I? Pretty please?"

"You better not. It would ruin your squeaky-clean reputation. But thanks for the offer."

"Man, you never let me have any fun," he said. I felt his grin against my cheek and smiled despite myself. "We should probably move. Mrs. Gilbert's going to have a cardiovascular event if we don't get on the bus."

"God, yes. I'm not much better than she is. The suspense is going to make me piddle."

He laughed and nuzzled my neck before releasing me. He didn't understand that I wasn't kidding about the piddling thing. This program was totally sweet; they selected a few seniors from area schools and paired us up with a bunch of physicians. We only got to shadow them for four half days, and I had a crazy huge stack of make-up work from my morning classes, but it was so worth it. If I was lucky, maybe they'd let me sit in on a few surgeries.

A few minutes later the bus pulled up to the health department, a squat brick building dwarfed by the medical complex surrounding it. I wanted to sprint inside but had to wait for Mrs. Gilbert, who clapped a lot faster than she walked.

The health department conference room was the exact color of Silly Putty, and it smelled like the inside of my gym locker. This failed to dull my excitement, though; I practically bounded into a seat. There were about ten other seniors there from St. Michael's and St. Joe's, the local Catholic schools. A few of them glared at the seven of us, like it was our fault that we were twenty minutes late.

The doctors waited at the front of the room in a single-file line of awesome; I barely restrained myself from falling at their feet and salaaming. As a distraction technique, I tried to figure out which ones were the surgeons. My two best bets were the woman with the razor-blade cheekbones and the man on the verge of hair gel overdose. Definitely not the hulking guy who reminded me of a shaved bear in a lab coat.

It probably wasn't smart to judge them based on appearance. I, for instance, was destined to be a world-renowned surgeon, but between my long brown braid, square-framed glasses, and boyish figure, I looked more like the kind of girl who works in a library and spends Friday nights having deep, meaningful conversations with her cats.

Of course, it didn't really matter. I didn't care which surgeon I got matched with, even if it was the hair-impaired bear. I was just looking forward to a week when I could babble about how cool medicine is without anyone looking at me funny. Aaron was usually the only person I could do that with, and even he had his limits.

Aaron sat on one side of me, chatting with Trey about basketball; the seat on my other side was empty until the bear man took it. He had to be almost seven feet tall and wasn't exactly thin. The folding chair creaked under the strain as he turned in my direction.

"Good morning," he said. "I'm Dr. Burr."

"Kate Grable."

His hand engulfed mine. His fingers had approximately the same circumference as my thighs, but his grip was surprisingly gentle. I began to reevaluate my earlier assessment. He totally had surgeon's hands.

His name didn't ring any bells, and I'd memorized the surgery listings on the Bayview Hospital website. I was just about to ask what kind of medicine he practiced when Mrs. Gilbert said, "Shall we start?"

I instantly developed butterflies in my stomach, along with an intense urge to throw my arms wide and scream "Finally! I've found my people!" I couldn't decide how that would be received, though, so I restrained myself and acted all blasé instead. I wasn't fooling anyone, but no one could say I wasn't trying my best.

"We all know why we're here," Mrs. Gilbert said, "and we're running a little late, so let's skip the formalities and get right on to the matches, shall we? Elle Dickensheets, Aaron Kingsman, and Trey Black, you'll be working with Dr. Dickensheets in orthopedics. Dr. Dickensheets?"

The hair gel addict stood up, displaying his laser-bleached teeth in what I assumed was supposed to be a smile. It didn't quite reach his eyes. But I could tell that Aaron was thrilled, because orthopedics was his first choice. He squeezed my hand and followed Dr. Dickensheets out of the room without looking back.

And the process went on. Pretty soon everyone was gone. Everyone except me, Mrs. Gilbert, and Dr. Burr.

"Kate," Mrs. Gilbert said, practically bouncing with excitement, "since you've got such a special background, we've got something unique planned for you that will give you more hands-on experience. Have you met Dr. Burr?"

I nodded, and Dr. Burr rumbled. Mrs. Gilbert took it as an affirmative response.

"Oh, good," she gushed. "Then I'll let you two get further acquainted. You don't need me, right? Of course you don't. Toodles."

She wiggled her fingers at us and hurried to the door.

"Excitable, isn't she?" Dr. Burr said after it closed behind her.

"Uh ... yeah." I knew I should wait for him to explain, but I had all the patience of a hyperactive squirrel. "So what kind of medicine do you practice?"

He scooted his chair around to face me and leaned over with his elbows on his knees. Now I could actually look him in the eyes instead of having to crank my neck back like I had a flip-top head. It was a definite improvement.

"Well," he said, "I'll be completely honest with you, Kate. I'm not in surgery. The surgeons tried to claim you based on your . . . ahem . . . clearly stated preferences. But I haven't had a student in two years, so I got first pick. I'd be honored to work with the girl who cured the zombie virus."

I felt both flattered at the compliment and disappointed at the lack of surgery in my future, and I knew that both showed on my face.

"All I ask is that you give me one day to introduce you to my work, and if you're not interested in staying, I'll let you go with Dr. Gonzalez," he told me. "She's head of surgery."

I couldn't turn down the offer without offending the giant physician with ursine tendencies, and that didn't seem like such a good idea. I swallowed the lump in my throat. "That sounds fair. What kind of medicine do you practice?"

He stood and smiled down at me from a ridiculous height. "I'm the county medical examiner."

Dr. Burr and I descended into the underbelly of the health department. We lived in a fairly small county, so the morgue was tucked into the basement instead of having its own building. Strangely enough, in all my medical-related stalking, I'd never been there, probably because you had to go through a labyrinth to find the darned thing. All our medical buildings were linked underground. This seemed like a great idea until you were alone in the tunnels at night and convinced that the corpses from the morgue were chasing you. Not that this had ever happened to me; I just had an overactive imagination and a history of random zombie attacks.

I scurried alongside Dr. Burr, taking about three steps to every one of his, while he kept up a steady stream of patter about how he was excited to have a student who wasn't going to puke for once. He wanted me to watch an autopsy, and if I was interested in staying, I could gown up and assist later in the week. I knew he was trying to bribe me, but with each second that passed, I minded this less and less. Any bribery that resulted in a scalpel in my hand was good bribery.

We reached the morgue doors; he walked up to the card swipe and started patting his pockets. All I could do was wait while he emptied a huge pile of gum wrappers and bits of paper onto the floor.

"Sorry," he said with a sheepish expression. "I think I lost my ID again."

He leaned on the intercom button until finally someone buzzed us in. We emerged into a huge chlorine-scented room covered floor to ceiling with tile. Four autopsy tables lined the back wall, and to our left stood a sink flanked by about seven hundred boxes of gloves and face masks. A guy was prepping a body in a closed autopsy suite to my right; I could see him through the oversized viewing window. He wore one of those supercool protective suits that made you look like a blueberry-flavored astronaut.

I wondered if they'd ever let me wear one. If so, I was definitely staying.

Dr. Burr held up a finger in my direction. "Just one second." Then he toggled the intercom so he could talk to the blueberry astronaut without opening the door.

I found it difficult to tear my eyes away from the body on the table. It was a man. He looked a little like my dad, only about ten years older and with an overgrown salt-and-pepper beard. His arms and legs stuck up in the air like he was just playing dead and might at any moment jump up and yell "Fooled ya!" The corpses on television were always arranged so prettily at autopsy. Either this one was defective or television had gotten things wrong again.

"This is Sebastian Black. Sebastian, Kate Grable," said Dr. Burr into the intercom. "Sorry we're late. I misplaced my card. I'll be there in about ten minutes if that works for you."

"No problem," came the reedy-voiced reply through the speaker. "This should be a quick one. I think it's Grable's disease. There's the usual dehydration of the extremities, and he's missing the tips of two fingers."

Sebastian's comment got my attention pretty quick. Grable's disease was the technical name for the zombie virus. It was named after me, so I felt a certain ownership of it. It had been three months since I'd found the cure and turned into instant-celebrity-just-add-zombie, but that kind of thing tends to stick with you. People treat you differently once you've been on CNN. Stupid but true.

"Grable's?" I asked. "But it's curable. Why is he working in the infectious suite?"

I could tell by his grin that Dr. Burr was impressed with my deductive abilities, but he didn't realize what a big geek I was. I knew lab procedures and basic equipment by heart.

"Oh, it's completely unnecessary from a medical standpoint. But sometimes we have to make concessions. We're still working against the fear factor," he said, waving a farewell to Sebastian and steering me toward a bank of offices at the far end of the room. "It's pretty customary for pathology assistants to insist on extreme precautions when dealing with a new disease. He'll chill out after a while."

The idea of more Grable's-related deaths made my stomach sink. I thought I'd saved the world, but that wasn't entirely true. The virus that had zombified our varsity football team hadn't been completely eradicated. The health department had made the cure widely available, but not everyone had come forward for treatment. For a while there, it hadn't been all that uncommon to see undead homeless people lurching down the street, and one of our cheerleaders had bitten three spectators and the opposing school's mascot at a basketball game a month earlier. But we hadn't had any new cases since she'd been treated. I had hoped it was finally over.

Dr. Burr read my expression all too easily. He reached under his paper-strewn desk, pulled out a can of Dr Pepper, and cracked it open.

"Here. You look like you could use a drink," he said.

It was lukewarm, and I didn't usually drink soda before ten, but this seemed like an ideal time to make an exception. I slugged down about half the can and imagined the caffeine whirling through my veins. It was an instant if imaginary high.

"All right." He started flipping through a tottering stack of three-ring binders. "Let's get you through the procedure manual pronto so we can move on to the interesting stuff. Do you want to watch the Grable's postmortem, or would you rather start with something that hits a little less close to home?"

"I absolutely want that one. I feel kind of obligated to observe, if you know what I mean."

He nodded. I honestly thought he got it. I also thought I'd end up spending my week with a bunch of dead people instead of in a surgery suite, and I was surprisingly excited about that. By all rights, I should have been rolling around on the floor in an ocean of surgery-deprived tears.

I heard a muted buzz from the main room and the doors swung open. Two uniformed police officers sauntered into the morgue. I wasn't surprised to see them; they were probably here to exchange witty banter and theories about their murder cases with the medical examiner.

"Dr. Burr?" one of the cops asked. He looked from the infectious suite to the office, trying to decide which way to go. Dr. Burr made it easy on him by walking out to meet them.

"I'm William Burr," he said agreeably. "What can I do for you?"

The cop held out a pair of handcuffs that glinted in the glare of the fluorescent lights like some wacked-out disco ball.

"You're under arrest for murder."

CHAPTER two

I t all happened so quickly. One minute I was sitting in Dr. Burr's office, planning all kinds of autopsy-related awesomeness. The next, he was in handcuffs and one of the cops was speeding through his Miranda rights like an auctioneer on uppers. It felt very Movie of the Week, but minus the sound track and scary Botoxed faces.

"Dr. Burr?" I said. My voice cracked despite my efforts to sound like the butt-kicking zombie killer the media seemed to think I was.

"I didn't murder anyone, Kate." He was surprisingly calm given that he was in the process of being arrested. "I'm sure this is just a misunderstanding."

"What can I do to help?"

The cop holding the cuffs shoved Dr. Burr toward the door before he could answer. Totally rude. And then when I started to follow, his partner clamped a hand down on my shoulder and held me back. Double rude.

"Kate?" Dr. Burr called out. "I want you to call—" The doors swung shut behind him. As far as marching orders went, they could have used a little improvement.

I squirmed out from under the cop's hand. "Would it have killed you to give us a minute?" I snapped. "I just started working here. I have no idea how to run a morgue."

"Who are you?" the cop asked.

"You don't recognize me? You're new, aren't you?"

I swear I wasn't being egotistical. It's just that I was the infamous zombie girl, and I'd resigned myself to the notoriety. People recognized me in the bathroom at restaurants these days, for god's sake. It just figured that my reputation failed me the one time I actually could have benefited from it.

"Why?" He tried to stare me down. It was kinda cute, actually. Not that I was interested, just less than intimidated. "Are you a criminal?"

"Of course not. My name's Kate," I said. He jotted it down. "Last name Grable."

He stopped writing.

"Kate Grable? The girl who cured the zombies?" he asked.

"Technically, zombies die and are then reanimated. People with Grable's disease aren't dead, unless you run them over with a car." I gulped and tried not to think too much about that. "It's an important distinction."

It's also important not to antagonize the police. Particularly if they've just arrested the guy with the power to put a scalpel in your hand and let you actually do something with it. But apparently I'd forgotten that. Whoops.

All he said was "Cool. Can I have your autograph?"

It was a chance to save face with the police, so I didn't laugh even though I really wanted to.

"Who should I make it out to?" I asked in my politest voice.

"Jordan. It's my first day." He puffed up proudly.

I scribbled, Jordan—Love and brains from the girl who cures zombies. Kate Grable. I immediately wanted to kill myself, because it sounded both flirty and ditzy. Time to change the subject before I made myself barf.

"You don't honestly think he killed somebody, do you?" I asked. "He's my new boss, kinda, and I'm not sure I want to work for a murderer."

He chucked me on the chin. So much for the flirty thing.

"Oh, it's him, all right. We haven't charged him yet, but it'll happen after all the analysis is complete. I'd bet my badge on it."

"You seem awfully sure."

I wasn't. After all, his badge was only a day old, so it wasn't much of a bet.

"His ID card was on the floor next to the body. And you should see this body! He's the only suspect with the physical size and strength to do this kind of damage."

"Where's the body now?"

He shrugged. "I dunno. Still at the scene, I suppose. Somebody's got to come pick it up."

I chewed furiously on my lower lip. It helped me to think. And it sounded like Dr. Burr needed all the lip chewing I could give him. "Are they calling somebody to investigate? What else can I do to help?"

"Don't worry, kid. We've got him. You can sit this one out."

I wanted to shave off his pitiful little goatee with a scalpel for calling me kid, but I let it pass. I was too busy brainstorming a hundred different scenarios to explain why Dr. Burr's ID might be at a murder scene.

"Thanks," I mumbled, because it seemed like I should say something.

He left. Maybe he said something first, but I wasn't exactly paying attention.

I hovered indecisively for a couple of minutes, torn between my obligation to clear Dr. Burr's name and my desire to get on with the surgical goodness. I knew I should call the school or maybe Mrs. Gilbert. They'd probably want to know that my mentor had just gotten arrested. But I wouldn't do it right away, because I wasn't going to pass up the opportunity to indulge my medical fantasies unchaperoned. This hadn't been on my list of expected outcomes. Sadly enough, I'd actually written a list of expected outcomes, like *Kate will actually use a real scalpel, and it will be awesome.* I had to stop that, because it clearly wasn't doing a bit of good.

A muted buzzing from the wall got my attention. I walked over and stabbed the intercom button with my finger like it had done something to offend me.

"Yeah?" I said.

The voice came back tinny and static-covered. "One to drop off."

"One what?"

An exasperated sigh. "A body."

"Oh! Of course. Just a sec."

I punched the button to open the doors, and a few moments later, two guys in black suits wheeled a body bag into the morgue. One of them gave me a sketchy little salute. "All right. Where do you want him?"

That was a good question. After a quick scan of the room, I jerked my thumb toward one of the aluminum autopsy tables, because my only other option was the floor. There must have been storage lockers around somewhere, but I didn't know where, and I wasn't about to exhibit my ignorance.

The delivery guys lifted the body onto the table. From the way they huffed and strained, it appeared the deceased was either overweight or had been carrying bricks in his pockets when he croaked. The moment the door buzzed shut behind them, I peeked. No bricks. No visible markings on the body either, just a balding middle-aged guy with a substantial beer belly. I was putting my money on heart disease. Now I just had to get Dr. Burr back so he could perform the autopsy and I could see if I was right.

The moment the door buzzed shut behind them, I ran for the infectious suite. Sebastian was still puttering around in there, completely oblivious to the whole arrest thing.

I flicked on the intercom.

"Hey," I said. He didn't notice, so I banged on the glass with my fist until he jumped. "Hey! Earth to Sebastian! We've got a problem."

It took me ten minutes to detach the roll and a half of duct tape Sebastian had used to secure his gloves to his suit, five minutes to get him out of the rest of the protective gear, two minutes to fill him in on the situation, and twenty to make him stop hyperventilating. I barely restrained myself from slapping him and telling him to man up.

Finally, he managed to get himself under control. I could tell he wasn't going to be much help. Sebastian wasn't much older than me. A college freshman, maybe? A sophomore at the most. He was one of those scrawny, haunted-looking types who get constantly shoved into toilets, and so thin that I wondered if he had pectus excavatum. I'd never seen a concave chest before. I was tempted to ask him to lift up his shirt, but something told me he'd take it the wrong way.

I'd just calmed him down. I didn't want to flip him out again.

"It's okay," I said, in the most soothing voice I could manage. "We can handle this, right? All we need to do is keep things under control until they release him. Is there an assistant medical examiner we can call?"

"Dr. Grundleford-Pluta. But she's vacationing on top of a mountain in Canada right now! I'm only a part-time college student; I can't run a morgue!"

He started flapping his hands madly at his sides, as if panic might have given him the ability to fly. I was starting to under-stand the toilet-shoving urge. I felt it right now, in fact.

"Don't panic. Leave Dr. Grundle-whatever a message and we'll see what she says." I held my hands up in a nonthreatening manner. "There's no need to fly south for the winter."

"What?" he wailed. "You're not making any sense."

"Don't worry about that. Think about Dr. Burr. He's counting on us."

"Is he going to jail?"

His lip quivered, and suddenly I felt bad for him.

"I don't know." It would probably make him panic again, but the guy deserved honesty at the very least. He was a medical professional. A hypersensitive, possibly concave medical profes-sional, but a professional nonetheless. "But I have another hour before I have to catch the bus back to school. Let's do as much as we can; I'm sure Dr. Burr will appreciate it."

"Okay." Having a concrete course of action seemed to steady him. "Why don't you help me check in the new guy?"

He jerked his thumb toward the body bag on the table, and I nodded eagerly. I must have seemed too chipper, because he looked at me funny. I made a mental note to quit bouncing in ex-citement whenever I was faced with a dead body. Because really, when I put it that way, it sounded creepy even to me.

And I made a mental note to rewatch some of the CSI epi-sodes I'd TiVoed when I got home. Because I might need the investigative tips if Dr. Burr didn't get released soon.

I didn't want to hunt down a murderer, but I'd do it if I had to.

CHAPTER

three

Sebastian and I made a good team when he wasn't hyper-ventilating. We got everything organized pretty fast. Then I lost track of time looking at some pathology slides under the micro-scope. When I glanced up at the clock, I realized I had a total of two minutes to get to the health department lobby. The only way I'd make it was if Sebastian had a stash of nuclear waste in his desk and I used it to mutate myself so I could break the sound barrier.

I grabbed my phone and dialed Aaron. He'd hold the bus for me, because he was the perfect boyfriend. Not that we didn't have our problems. Every time we argued, I panicked. He was the first guy I'd ever dated, after all, and over the past few months, I'd be-come aware of how little I knew about relationships. I had this nagging worry that eventually he would come to his senses and realize he belonged with someone with better social skills. And boobs.

The phone rang and rang. I'd resigned myself to voice mail when he finally picked up.

"Aaron!" I threw on my coat and scarf and waved a frantic goodbye to Sebastian. "Don't let them leave without me, okay? You won't believe what happened; I'll tell you once I get there."

"Hey, babe," he replied. "Where are you? Aren't you late?"

"Yeah, I'm late. Haven't you noticed?"

"Sorry, I hadn't looked at the time," he said. I heard a burst of shrill girlish laughter in the background. It made me want to put out my eardrums with my thumbs. "Listen, you better get here fast. The bus just pulled in."

And then he hung up on me.

Aaron had never hung up on me before.

My knee-jerk reaction was to panic, because the hyena laughter plus hang-up wasn't a good combo. But as I rushed down the hallway, I reminded myself that Aaron wasn't that kind of guy. He wasn't hooking up with random laughing girls in the health department lobby; his cell had probably dropped the call. Besides, it seemed pretty petty to be obsessing over guys when there was a murderer on the loose and my mentor was in jail.

I sped out of the elevator, nearly getting run over by a gurney in the process. But the breathless dash was totally worth it when I flew into the lobby and saw the bus parked outside. I speed-walked toward it, scanning the small group of students clustered just inside the doors, taking shelter from the wind.

Someone stepped in front of me. "Have you seen Aaron Kingsman?" I asked before I realized it was Trey. "Oh. Hi."

"Hey, Kate," he said, licking his lips. Maybe they were chapped. I really wanted them to be, because the alternative was gross. "How's it goin'?"

"Have you seen Aaron?" I repeated. He scowled, and I threw up my hands. "What? It's not like I'm asking for the square root of pi; I just need to find my boyfriend. What's your problem?"

Before he could answer, I heard Aaron's voice. "Kate!" Trey and I both turned to see him standing just a few feet away. "What's going on?"

"I was just going to ask Kate if she had any Chap Stick." Trey's face relaxed into his usual easy grin. "Do you have any, bro?"

Aaron was always prepared for everything; he opened his backpack and rummaged around. It was so good to see him, and now I felt kind of silly for assuming he was going to dump me all because of a stupid phone call. I was overcome with a potent wave of embarrassment at my neurotic wackjob tendencies, but then I noticed the girl standing next to him and nearly tripped over my own feet.

She was freakishly, annoyingly cute, and she seemed to think everyone in the world was interested in seeing her cleavage. Every time she moved, she led with her boobs. She thrust those things out so far that she'd throw her back out if she wasn't careful. I would have warned her, but her breasts were primarily aimed at my boyfriend, so she deserved a slipped disk or two. Or seven.

"Hey, babe." Aaron straightened up, smiling at me. "The bus driver just left to look for you. I think she's pretty pissed."

I mentally reassured myself that he still publicly acknowledged our relationship and focused on the matter at hand. "She'll have to deal," I said. "My doctor left me in charge of the morgue for a while. I couldn't just leave. The corpses might rise again."

"If anyone else said that, I'd laugh." He slung an arm over my shoulder. "Hey, I almost forgot. Elle, this is Kate. Kate, this is Elle. Elle's a senior at St. Michael's. She's shadowing in orthopedics with me and Trey."

"Nice to meet you," Elle said, but she didn't even look at me. She was too busy rubbing up against my boyfriend's shoulder. He kept edging away from her, but she wasn't taking the hint. I instantly disliked her.

"Dude." Trey nudged Aaron's arm, totally ignoring Elle and me. "What's up with this crap weather? Back home in SoCal, I would have been surfing right about now."

"Man, that sounds good," Aaron said. "I bet you used to go all the time."

"Yeah, there was this one time me and the guys made this bet. . . ."

This story bored me already, so I turned my attention to Elle. She kept tossing her hair around like her head was full of helium. This girl had the body of a blow-up doll and the brains of your average Barbie.

"So, Kate," she chirped. "Are you like Aaron's sister or something?"

I waited for Aaron to correct her, but he was listening to Trey tell some idiotic story about how it's never a good idea to surf naked. Still, I was kind of pissed that she didn't already know he was taken.

"Actually, I'm his girlfriend," I said.

The words were only halfway out of my mouth when she chirped, "Well, we just hit it off so well that Aaron invited me to double-date with you tomorrow."

He turned back to us and gave my shoulder a squeeze. "Yeah, is that okay with you, Kate?"

Aaron and I had a standing dinner date with my best friend Rocky and her boyfriend, Bryan, on Wednesdays, because it was the only night free for all of us. Between Rocky's show choir, my Quiz Bowl, and Aaron's track practice, our schedules were tough to coordinate. It was something special for the four of us to do together, and I couldn't believe Aaron had invited some girl he'd just met, but I couldn't say no. Then I'd be the bad guy.

"Sure." I pasted a smile on my face. "Maybe Trey here could be your date." I grabbed him by the arm and displayed him like this was a game show and she'd just won the grand prize. Neither of them looked particularly happy to be shoved together like that. I couldn't keep from grinning.

"That's a great idea!" Aaron said.

Then our bus driver flounced up. I knew her well; she drove me to school most mornings, which was the height of humili-

26

ation given that I was a senior. I couldn't drive because of my seizures. I'm an epileptic, and I had to be seizure-free for six months before they'd let me back on the road again. I had about three and a half months of misery left before I got my car back.

"Kate." The driver scowled at me. "Sandi-with-an-i is super-pissed that you're so late."

She constantly referred to herself in the third person. It was just one of the many reasons why I considered the bus to be the physical manifestation of hell itself.

"Sorry," I said. "My doctor kept me over."

"Tell it to Mr. Dryer. He'll want to know why we're late for fifth period, and Sandi-with-an-i is not taking the blame."

"Fine."

I looked over Aaron's shoulder just in time to see Elle boarding the St. Michael's bus. She blew a kiss at the back of his head. Or maybe she was blowing a kiss at me. I wasn't sure which would be worse.

Aaron followed me up the grimy steps onto the bus, and by the look on his face when he slid onto the cracked leather seat next to me, he knew I wasn't exactly pleased. We bounced around for a couple of minutes in silence before he finally said, "So what's wrong?"

I took a deep breath, folded my arms so he wouldn't see my hands shake, and plunged in. "I had a bad day. And . . . you know I don't have a lot of experience with this whole dating thing, so I'm going to come right out and ask: what's up with Elle?"

He arched a brow. "We're sharing a doctor, so Trey and I got to hang with her all day. She seems pretty nice."

"So there's nothing going on? Because she seemed really interested in you. And I'm trying not to be all jealous and clingy, but I could use a little reassurance here."

"She was flirting with me pretty hard most of the morning, so I brought you up in conversation like four times. But if you think she didn't get the picture, I can be more explicit. It's just that . . ." He winced. "She's Dr. Dickensheets's daughter. I've got to be careful. If I piss her off and she tells her dad I'm a dick, it could ruin my chances of getting a good recommendation. I need it if I'm going to get off the wait list at Cornell."

"Dickensheets? That's probably the most ridiculous name in the history of the world. You'd think they'd change it."

He snorted. "Yeah. So do you understand the dilemma here?"

"Honestly?" I took a deep breath. "I guess I can't blame you for being in a sucky situation. I'm sorry. I hate being high-maintenance. Like I said, I'm really stressed. And I'm not so good at this relationship thing. I'm much better with fungal infections."

"You have no idea how hot that is."

I couldn't figure out if he was kidding. His grin suggested he was, but the kiss that followed was awfully serious. Mrs. Gilbert had to separate us.

We pulled up to the school shortly thereafter. Mr. Dryer stood at the front doors, glowering at the bus in general and me in particular. After Sandi-with-an-i explained why we were tardy, he let everyone else go to class while he escorted me to his minuscule office. We didn't exactly get along, Mr. Dryer and I. He was a high school vice principal, and he had a mullet. I think that pretty much says it all right there.

In his office, he proceeded to read me the riot act, which consisted of the usual blah-blah about respect for the rules, courtesy to my fellow students, and the need to make a good impression on the FDA people. That took a good ten minutes, because he got really worked up and paced back and forth behind the desk even though it was only three steps in each direction. It made me dizzy.

"Do you have anything to say for yourself?" he finished, folding his arms over his scrawny chest.

This was the moment. I should have told him Dr. Burr had been arrested, and then he would have reassigned me to a surgeon and the world would have been right again. But I didn't want to do that. Maybe I'd have a chance to check out that murder victim tomorrow. Maybe I'd notice something the experts hadn't. It sounded egotistical, but it had happened before.

"I'm sorry, Mr. Dryer," I said, keeping a straight face with some effort. "I understand how important this is, but the pathology department hasn't had a student in ages, and they were awfully backed up. But we should be caught up tomorrow, so this won't happen again."

He blinked. "Well, okay. I . . . appreciate your candor. If you'll promise not to be late again, I won't report this to Mrs. Gilbert."

"Absolutely."

He dismissed me. I walked out of the office wondering where I'd left my brains. My top two bets were somewhere in the morgue, where they'd fit right in, or in Elle Dickensheets's cleavage, where they wouldn't. I'd just thrown away a chance to get everything I wanted. For a genius, I sure was stupid.

By the time I made it through the lunch line, all the pizza was gone. The other option was goulash, and that wasn't an option at all. I ended up with a carton of chocolate milk and a cardboard bowl full of fries. Usually, I grabbed a Coke from my locker, but thanks to Mr. Dryer, I hadn't had time. I could already feel the beginnings of a caffeine headache at my temples.

When I made my way through the packed cafeteria over to the cheerleader table, my friend Kiki scowled at me. Kiki was good at everything—she was head varsity football cheerleader, vice president of student council, this year's homecoming queen, and a top contender for salutatorian. But she didn't do angry well. It was like a bunny trying to be intimidating—it would never work. So I just smiled, tugged on a bouncy blond curl, and sat down next to her.

"Hey, you." I shook my milk. "Sorry, the bus got back late, and then Mr. Dryer talked at me for like fifteen minutes."

The angry look vanished from her face. "I was thinking you stood me up. What did Mullet Man have to say?"

"Nothing worth repeating. So did you look at the Rockathon sign-up?"

"Yeah, and I only had a few changes. Mindi and Kellan are on the outs right now, so you might want to move him to a different time slot. . . ."

I scarfed down fries while she ran through my volunteer list. Before they'd set the dates for the FDA program, I'd decided to put on a Rockathon fund-raiser for the Epilepsy Foundation. It seemed pretty easy. Get a few rocking chairs, take pledges, and sign people up to rock all night long. Of course, the two activities ended up being scheduled during the same week, but by the time I found out, it was too late to change the date for the fund-raiser, and I wasn't just going to cancel it. The Rockathon would help me stand out from the premed crowd. Curing the zombie virus had helped me get into a good program—but it didn't make me a lock for med school.

It was a good thing I had Kiki, because without her magical powers of recruitment, there was no way I could have filled all the slots. We had shifts of two people signed up to rock for an hour each, from Friday at six p.m. all the way to Saturday at noon. And Rocky had arranged for the show choir to do a rock-and-roll medley, and the cheerleaders would be selling concessions. Between the Rockathon pledges and concessions, we'd probably rake in about five thousand dollars. Thank god for my friends, because without their help, I probably would have raised four. As in four dollars.

Kiki had offered to rearrange the schedule to make sure that people paired to rock together got along and no blood was spilled. It was just one of the many things she'd done to make this thing work, even though it hadn't been her idea in the first place. I really appreciated that. But while she was running all the changes by me, I couldn't stop thinking about Aaron and Elle and Dr. Burr and the mysterious murder victim. I wondered if they'd released any information about the deceased yet; maybe I could swing by the library and look it up online. I probably had time to do it before the end of lunch if I left right away.

Kiki folded the list and handed it over with a smile.

"I owe you big-time for this, Keeks," I said. "And I really want to hang with you, but I need to do a little emergency research in the library before class starts. Can we catch up later?"

"Emergency?" She knew me well enough to take me seriously. "I'll walk with you. Anything I can do to help?"

"I don't really know what I'm doing to help."

I told her all about it as we climbed the stairs to the third floor, where they'd hidden our library. It was pretty empty at this time of day; Mrs. Wilson was helping a mousy freshman girl in the biography section, and she raised a hand to greet us as we passed but didn't bother us. I'd spent plenty of time in here; she knew I didn't need supervision. And Kiki was . . . well, Kiki.

"That's really terrible," she whispered as we made our way to the computer bank at the back of the room. "I can't believe you didn't run screaming in the other direction. I mean, if Dr. Burr comes back, won't you be wondering if he really is a murderer?"

I shrugged. "He doesn't scare me. If you turned him into a vampire and sent him after me, then I might be scared."

"Please don't say things like that." She snickered under her breath. "It makes me tempted to go stake shopping."

"Don't worry. Even after everything I've seen and done, I still don't believe in vamps."

"Reassuring."

I sat down at the computer on the end, typed in my student ID number, and started searching. The *Gazette* website didn't have any info, so I tried the local Fox news station. All I could find there was this completely useless story:

```
Bayville police are investigating a homicide
that occurred last night in the City Grille
parking lot. The victim's identity is being
withheld pending notification of the family.
```

I scowled. "Well, that's no help at all."

Kiki leaned down to get a better look at the screen. "What did you find?"

When I glanced up, I noticed a blur of movement in the air behind her, like a giant hummingbird had broken into the library and was checking out the reference materials.

"Wha—"

Kiki started to turn, but everything happened so fast. I didn't even get the word out before the flying mystery object slammed into the side of her head. She let out a grunt and toppled right on top of me, clocking my nose with her elbow and knocking my glasses off. Tears filled my eyes; I half fell, half slid out of my chair.

"What the hell?" I gasped.

Another projectile flew toward me. I batted at it wildly, and it struck my forearm and fell into my lap with a thump. My arm went instantly numb. That was inconvenient but probably preferable to screaming in pain. We were in a library, after all. Screaming was not encouraged.

I could see a tan-colored blur crouched over near the reference books, and it launched another red projectile at me. My choices were pretty limited. I could call for Mrs. Wilson, but she'd just gotten back to school after being out for a month after her heart attack. She would have been just one more person to protect.

In my lap was the encyclopedia that had nearly obliterated my arm. It was time to give this idiot a taste of his own medicine. I threw it as hard as I could. Details were still indistinct, between my lack of corrective lenses and the watery eyes, but I didn't need to score a direct hit. I just wanted to scare him off. So as soon as that one was in the air, I grabbed the one that had clocked Kiki and threw that too.

I had no idea if I was hitting the guy or not, but he wasn't throwing any more books at us. Kiki groaned and rolled into my lap with her head clasped in her hands.

"That hurt!" she wailed.

"Stay down!" I hissed, grabbing another book. But by the time I cocked my arm to throw, the fuzzy figure was gone.

It took only a minute of groping around on the table to locate my glasses. When I finally found them, I wished I hadn't. Mrs.

Wilson stood over near the reference books, wearing a tan tweed jacket, a matching skirt, and an expression of pure horror. Had I just flung a Britannica at her head?

"Kate Grable, what on earth are you doing?" she exclaimed, looking at the damaged books strewn across the floor.

"I'm sorry! I was just..." I trailed off. Something told me she didn't care about the book-flinging bandit, and anything else I said would only get me into more trouble. "I'm sorry," I said again.

That was how I ended up in Mr. Dryer's office for the second time that day. At least this time Kiki was with me, and she stood firm by my side.

"Vandalism of school property will not be tolerated," Mr. Dryer announced, pacing again. The front of his mullet was wilting. "I am quite disappointed with you both."

"We already told you," Kiki said with more patience than I'd ever had. "Someone threw a book at me hard enough to knock me out. You can feel the dent in my head if you want. Kate was just protecting me."

"So you're telling me that you were in the library, minding your own business, when someone started chucking books at you?"

"That's exactly what we're telling you!" I said.

"Then why didn't Mrs. Wilson see anyone else in the library?" he asked.

"Maybe they snuck in while she was helping another student?" I shrugged. "Or they were already in the library when we got there. It wouldn't be too tough to hide in the stacks."

He shook his head. "Well, that's neither here nor there. You two were caught damaging school property. If you could identify the third student, that might be different. But as it stands, you'll be spending this week in detention, and you're lucky to only get that."

I felt the blood drain from my face. I'd already gotten accepted to all the premed programs I'd applied for, but would this change my eligibility? I was pretty sure it wouldn't, but pretty sure wasn't completely sure.

"Mr. Dryer!" I exclaimed, jumping to my feet. I would have said more, but Kiki grabbed my arm and squeezed.

"We understand," she said, her fingers wrapped around my forearm. "And we didn't mean to damage school property. If we find the person who threw the books at us, would you reconsider the punishment?"

He made a big show of considering this, stroking his chin thoughtfully. "I'll give due consideration to any evidence, Miss Carlyle."

"Thank you." She tugged me toward the door.

I kicked the wall after we got outside. Not hard enough to hurt anything, but I figured if I was going to get detention for damaging school property, I might as well earn it.

Kiki took off toward the secretaries to get a hall pass, so I had to scramble to catch up. "Did that really happen?" I asked. "Because it all feels like a bad dream."

"Oh, I'll tell you what happened." She rubbed the back of her head, and now she really looked mad. "I think I caught a glimpse of the guy before he creamed me with that dictionary, and he's going to find out that nobody messes with me. Or my friends."

She got out her cell, flipped the keypad open, and started typing furiously.

"What are you doing?" I hissed, moving in front of her to hide the illegal phone use.

"Sending out an alert to the squad," she said. "By the end of next period, I'll have a list of guys with brown facial hair"

"Was that brown blur a beard? It was hard for me to tell without the glasses."

Kiki nodded. "We can go over the list of suspects in detention."

"And when we find out who attacked us," I said, "he's going to wish he hadn't."

"Oh, he's going to wish he was dead," she said. By the look on her face, she was only half joking.

CHAPTER four

By the time I plopped down in front of the television that night with a grilled cheese and a Coke, I was exhausted. I'd managed to get through a few calculus assignments in detention, but otherwise the whole thing was a wash. Kiki's cheerleading spies had only located two guys in the entire school with enough facial hair to be suspect—Mr. Lutner, who had been teaching Spanish conjugations fifth period, and Jacob Kleinfelter, who had been verified as present in shop class. Mindi Skibinski checked the visitor's log for us while she was volunteering in the office, and the only visitor signed in at that time was named Gertrude. I was willing to bet she wasn't bearded.

The obvious conclusion was that the beard must have been a disguise. This left us with no way to identify the guy. If it really had been a guy.

I'd been obsessing over it for hours without any results, so I finally gave up. I turned on a CSI rerun and took my frustrations out on my sandwich.

"Whatcha watching?"

My dad brushed crumbs off the floral couch fabric and plopped down next to me.

I glanced up at the screen, which was filled with a montage of techies hard at work in various laboratory settings. "CSI." I shrugged.

"You're frustrated," he said.

I swallowed. "How can you tell?"

"I've never seen you scowl at a guy in a lab coat before. Anything I can help with?"

"Well...you could sign this form from school. Somebody chucked a bunch of books at me and Kiki, and then he ran off, and they're blaming us for the mess. I got detention. You've got to sign off to prove that I told you I'm a delinquent." The corners of my mouth turned down uncontrollably. I felt like I'd crack if one more thing went wrong.

"You did what?" His eyebrows jumped so far up his forehead that I thought they might pop off and run for cover.

I told him all about it, dwelling extensively on the part where Kiki was knocked unconscious by volume 13 of the Encyclopedia Britannica. He cut me off somewhere around the part where I was heroically shielding her defenseless body with my own.

"Well, that sucks," he said. "So will you still be able to come pick Mom up from the airport on Thursday?"

"Yeah, if you pick me up at school. Her plane gets in at six, right?"

He nodded. "Good. And it sounds like you made the right choice, regardless of what that idiot vice principal thinks. Detention isn't the end of the world, so long as you don't make a habit of it. I once got detention for toilet-papering the school."

His voice got all dreamy, like flinging rolls of double ply was one of the highlights of his high school experience, and I braced myself for a long and drawn-out story about the good old days. I wished I'd brought down my copy of Crime and Punishment, because I had to finish it for Lit and it would have made a great excuse. But I hadn't.

When the doorbell rang, I nearly applauded.

"Sorry, Dad," I said. "I think Jonah's still at his gaming thing, so I better get that."

He leaned back and cleaned his glasses on the edge of his sweater. "I'll be here."

I opened the door to see Detective Despain on my front step, and my heart sank. Her lips were pressed into a flat line that I remembered all too well; they didn't seem to fit on her china-doll face. Despain had been my main contact at the police department after the whole zombie thing went down. I liked her. She treated me like a real person instead of just a teenager.

"Kate," she said gently. "I'm sorry to bother you."

"What's wrong?" I gasped, bracing myself against the doorframe. "Who's hurt?"

"It's okay." Dad came up behind me and put his hands on my

shoulders. I imagined the worst. Mom's plane had crashed. One of Jonah's stupid friends had driven off the road and the car blew up. Something horrible. "I would have called, but I wasn't sure if you were home, Phil, and I know Kate still doesn't have her license back yet. I knew she would want to come."

"Come where?" I asked.

"The conference center. Jonah found a murder victim, and he's a little shaken up."

"Another one?" I said.

She nodded. From the wide-eyed expression on her face, I could tell that Jonah wasn't the only one who was shaken.

Dad and I followed Despain's police cruiser to the convention center. On one hand, she'd repeatedly reassured us that Jonah was fine while we threw on coats and hunted for our gloves. On the other, she drove with the flashers on. So I wasn't sure how worried I should be, and I white-knuckled it the whole way.

Our so-called convention center really wasn't all that impressive. Bayview had one hotel right off the highway; it had a convention wing with a couple of small meeting rooms and a ballroom. Any school dance that wasn't held in the gym ended up there by default. In a small town like ours, they didn't get a lot of business, so when the local role-playing club requested permission to hold a gaming night there on Tuesdays, they'd said yes.

When we got there, Despain bypassed the main hotel entrance, but I could see the lobby as we followed her around to the side of the building. It was full of teenagers and college students sporting latex elf ears, pointy wizard hats, and chain-mail bikinis. The thought alone made me chafe.

Yellow crime scene tape blocked off the twin glass doors that led into the convention center. It fluttered in the stiff wind, one end working its way loose and waving toward us like a monstrous Day-Glo tentacle. But maybe that was just my hyperactive imagination at work.

Despain ducked the tape and held the door open for us. I walked in without pausing; I knew the layout pretty well already. Before I'd lost my driving privileges, I'd had to pick Jonah up here a few times. Large events like the live-action role-playing were in the ballroom, smaller ones like tabletop and miniature games in the conference rooms. The first door on the left led to the ballroom; I looked inside and saw a couple of cops questioning a tired-looking guy in jeans, a T-shirt, and full Klingon makeup. I didn't get the appeal of the bulgy forehead, but then again, I went squealy over viral cultures. I couldn't exactly make accusations of weirdness.

"Jonah's in the second room. The body's in the third." Despain pointed toward one of the larger conference rooms, which was hung with banners proclaiming it the MEDIEVAL JOUSTING ARENA. "Have you eaten recently, Kate? If it's okay with your dad, I'd like you to take a look at the deceased for me. I need a future-professional opinion."

Dad nodded absentmindedly, but I didn't think he'd heard a thing she said after my brother's name. He made a beeline for the second conference room. When he went through the door,

Jonah immediately started shouting so loud you could probably have heard him from space. "Dad, you should have seen it! That was so wicked!"

I let out a breath I didn't even know I was holding. I should have known he'd be fine; he actually enjoyed stuff like this. He'd gotten so excited about the zombies that he'd nearly peed himself.

Despain was waiting for me outside the yellow-taped murder scene. "You want me to look at the murder victim?" I asked. I couldn't decide whether to feel flattered or sick. "He's not a zombie, is he?"

"No. But it's . . . weird. And with that mess last fall, you've shown that you can think outside the box. I know it's a lot to ask, and I'd probably get into big trouble if my boss found out about this, but . . ." She swallowed, and again I saw that tight-eyed expression. I didn't like it. "This guy is killing kids, Kate. I'll do whatever I have to in order to catch the bastard."

"You don't have to convince me," I said. "I want to help."

"Thank you," she said. "Let me introduce you to our victim."

She led me into the so-called jousting room. The body was impossible to miss, because it was smeared across most of the floor. One look and my stomach threatened to rebel. Yeah, I'd seen dead bodies before, but that didn't mean I had to like it.

Maybe it would be best to ease into this. I let my eyes roam the floor. There was plenty of blood and yuck, which didn't exactly surprise me. But the tile was also dotted with chunks of white . . . something. Lots of it. My curiosity won out over my gag reflex, and I knelt down to get a closer look.

"What's this white stuff?" I asked, pointing.

"Coconut."

I must have looked at her like she was crazy; she pointed over my shoulder. I turned to see a row of potted palms dripping with coconuts.

"What the . . . ?" I said.

"What?" Despain was instantly at my side. "Does that mean something to you?"

"No. But I'd sure like to know what kind of idiot thinks coconuts are native to medieval Europe. This is supposed to be the jousting room, after all."

"That is weird." She sat back on her heels. "Particularly since I think a coconut was the murder weapon."

CHAPTER
five

I stood in the middle of a crime scene, contemplating a deadly coconut. Of all the things I'd expected to see today, lethal fruit wasn't one of them.

"Well," I said slowly, "I guess we can rule out premeditated murder."

"Why do you say that?" Detective Despain asked.

"Can you imagine someone lugging a coconut around intending to bludgeon someone with it? If I intend to kill somebody, I'm going to grab a knife or a gun. Not a fuzzy fruit that people use to make tropical drinks."

She nodded. "I came to the same conclusion."

I felt a swell of pride but immediately pushed it away. I'd let my ego blind me during the whole zombie thing; I sure as heck wasn't going to do it again.

"All right," I said. "I'm ready to look at the victim now."

Despain took me by the elbow. She wasn't exactly dragging me, just applying a firm pressure that made me feel a little steadier. Like she knew this would be hard and she had my back. I appreciated the support. But still? I was so not prepared for the condition of the body.

I saw the face first. Completely unmarked. Well, except for the fancy tattoos like scrollwork around the eyes. She had pointy elf ears and purple hair. My stomach sank; she was definitely a gamer. I just hoped Jonah didn't know her; his part in the zombie annihilation squad had made him strangely popular with the geek-girl crowd. I didn't want to be the one to tell him one of his groupies had been murdered. But thankfully, he didn't seem to have recognized her.

Unfortunately, the rest of the body wasn't so pristine. From the neck down, there was an explosion of gore and coconut bits. I was never buying an Almond Joy again.

The right side of her torso was caved in, the ribs broken and sticking out through the skin. Her limbs were twisted in unnatural directions. Her right arm looked like a big question mark, which would have been funny if it wasn't, you know, an arm. I couldn't imagine anyone strong enough, not to mention insane enough, to do this.

"What do you think?" Despain gave my arm a squeeze. "Coconuts, right?"

I swallowed with difficulty. Of course it figured that my med-geek tendencies would desert me at a time like this. Despain actually wanted my professional opinion, and all I could think of was that the victim wasn't much older than me.

"Kate?" Despain tugged on my sleeve. "Maybe this was a mistake."

"I can do this." I shook her off irritably. "You asked for my help, let me give it."

She backed off. I should have probably felt guilty over snapping at her, but I was pretty sure she already understood I was just angry at whoever had done this.

I turned back to the body. Her getup was so darned distracting. She had this huge medallion at her throat covered in red and yellow gems too bright to be anything other than painted glass. That wasn't so bad. But the hints of unmarked skin were painted, or maybe tattooed, in a scale pattern. I couldn't figure out what she was supposed to be. A dragon elf lady? Then again, I couldn't understand a lot of things. Like reality TV. And most teenage boys.

"I'm not so sure, Detective Despain. You see that . . . gouge there?" I asked, pointing. "And there? A coconut's fairly flat. But this looks like she was stabbed, or . . ." I gulped. I didn't want to say this out loud.

"Or what?"

"I think those might be claw marks."

"And then they beat her with the coconut to obscure the damage?"

All of a sudden, I didn't want to look at her anymore. "Maybe." My hands were shaking. "Can we go out in the hall now?"

*　*　*

I slid down the wall to sit on the floor with my legs stretched halfway across the hallway. Despain hadn't wanted to leave me, but she had a job to do. Right now, she was checking to see if there were any witnesses other than Jonah. I needed the time to get a hold of myself anyway. Maybe the killer would happen to run out this way and I'd trip him, and then it would all be over. Since I was wishing for things, I wanted a new med kit too. And maybe a pony.

But the only person who came out was Jonah. His narrow face was flushed with excitement, and his hair stuck out over his elf ears. For god's sake, the guy was wearing a pair of tights under his tunic. As if he didn't look geeky enough already. One look at him and people wanted to stick his head into toilets. Most people, anyway.

"Kate," he said solemnly, "I have had another brush with death, and it was *awesome*."

"I'm glad you're okay." I sounded just as weary as I felt. "But I don't think some girl getting killed is particularly awesome. It could have been you."

He sank down next to me, his shoulder touching mine. And yeah, he was swirly-compatible, but he'd also stood with me against some tough odds before. It felt better just having him there, although I would have vehemently denied it in public.

"You don't need to worry about me, Kate. But yeah, it's sad about Holly."

"Did you know her?" I sat up straighter. "Who did she hang

out with? Did she have any enemies? When was she last seen alive?"

"Slow down!" he said, waving his hands at me. "I didn't know her very well. She was the priestess of the Clan of Awesome. I run Nightdark Clan. We run in totally different circles, but if you hang around here long enough, you learn most people's names."

I slumped back down in defeat. Man, nothing was going my way.

A door slammed somewhere down the hallway. I was more than a little jumpy, what with the whole dead-body-in-the-other-room thing, and I barely restrained myself from leaping to my feet with my arms held up like I knew kung fu, which I most certainly did not. My neck prickled; my hands trembled with the adrenaline rush. Stupid, really, because it was probably just another cop. Or a Klingon. Someone like that. They'd turn the corner any second now, and then I'd berate myself for stupidity.

It wasn't another cop.

It was a tiny old woman in a navy blue suit. Her skin was the approximate color and texture of beef jerky. Normal people don't look like that; I had an immediate, intense zombie flashback. At least this one was kind of small.

"Jonah." I elbowed him, pointing toward the undead creature shambling toward us.

"What?" He blinked, looking down the hall. "Aw, crap. Another one?"

"Hey, guys," I cupped my hand in front of my mouth, calling toward the ballroom. "We got a Grable's case out here."

One of the cops would come and neutralize her, but I didn't want to wait. Bite marks really itch when they're healing, and I had had enough of them on my arms and legs to last the rest of my life.

We scrambled to our feet. As we backed away, I looked around desperately for some kind of protective weapon. Unfortunately, weaponry is a little scarce in the middle of a convention center hallway.

"Here!" Jonah hissed, pointing toward a door marked with a gold plaque—SUPPLY CLOSET.

I followed him inside as the zombie advanced toward us. It was one of the creepier ones I'd seen. She looked like one of Santa's elves after it got left under the broiler just a little too long.

The door slammed behind us, leaving us in pitch-blackness. "Weapons," I muttered, groping around for something defensive. My hand searched the shelves to my right. Toilet paper. Lots of it. Something told me it wouldn't do much good to pelt the zombie with rolls of Angel Soft. I heard a clatter and a muffled "Crap," from Jonah. He evidently wasn't having much better luck than I was.

Finally, I found a broom and held it out in front of me in a pseudodefensive position.

The door swung open. I didn't wait; I gave that crispy critter a face full of bristles. "Go away, zombie!" I yelled. Jonah had my back; he pelted her with rolls of paper towels. One bounced off her forehead. She yelped and backpedaled. Then I noticed the uniformed cop standing by her side. It was the same guy who'd asked for my autograph earlier.

"Stop that!" the zombie said irritably, trying to shove the broom away from her face.

Zombies don't talk like normal people. It was hard to believe that this woman was a regular old human, but all evidence pointed in that direction. Unfortunately, Jonah had already launched another paper towel missile at her face. I swatted it away with my broom.

"Um, sorry," I said. "We thought you were . . ."

"A zombie. Yes, I heard." Her leathery face screwed up with distaste. "I'm the hotel manager. Is that why you're ransacking my supply closet? I thought you were trying to loot us."

"No, ma'am," said Jonah, laying on what little charm he had. "We're sorry, but it was an honest mistake. We'll clean up the mess."

"You'd better," she said. "Or I'll have you arrested. No one vandalizes my building while I'm on the job!" Then she lurched back down the hallway, muttering to herself.

The cop leaned against the doorframe and watched as we straightened all the shelves, chuckling the entire time. I wanted to pelt him with toilet paper, but with my luck, I'd probably get arrested, so I didn't.

CHAPTER

six

I showed up at the morgue the next day with circles under my eyes and a cup of coffee as big as my head. Sandi-with-an-i had tried to take the coffee away from me when I got on the bus, but one look at my face scared her off. I got way more satisfaction out of that than I should have.

One step through the door and I knew Dr. Burr hadn't been released from jail yet. Sebastian sat in the middle of the tile floor, letting out little goatlike bleats of panic every five seconds. I felt a sudden wave of pity. Yeah, he was annoying, but his boss had been arrested for murder. I remembered how horrible it had felt when I'd learned that someone I respected had betrayed my trust.

So instead of biffing him on the head with a notebook and telling him to suck it up, I sat down cross-legged on the floor and chucked him on the shoulder.

"Come on," I said gently. "It'll be okay. We can handle things until someone shows up to help."

"But there's nobody to help! Dr. Grundleford-Pluta is unreachable, and Dr. Burr is gone, and we've got two murder victims, and three bodies from the hospital, and we're going to run out of spaces in storage, and I don't know what to do, and—"

I patted his back, maybe a little more forcefully than I should have, but the effort had to count for something.

"That stuff is out of our control. Let's focus on what we *can* control."

"I wish Dr. Burr were here."

"Me too." We sat in companionable silence for a minute. "So what's it like working with him, anyway? He seems like such a gentle, patient guy."

"He's not a murderer, if that's what you're getting at," Sebastian snapped, his panic morphing abruptly into anger. "It's what you really want to know, isn't it?"

"Chill, okay? I find it tough to believe too. He just doesn't seem like the type."

I used my nicest voice, but it didn't have any effect on him. Sebastian had suddenly turned into a thug in geek's clothing. It was almost laughable, except he seemed serious.

"Yeah, and I'm sure you're an expert on crimes of passion," he said, glowering.

"I'm agreeing with you, Sebastian. Why are you trying to pick a fight with me?"

This time, I went for logic; I was better at that than the

touchy-feely garbage. It seemed to get through too. I watched all the fuss and bluster melt away. I could actually see him shrink back to normal size. Kinda like the Hulk, only less colorful.

"Sorry," he muttered. "I'm sorry. I'm just . . . pissed, I guess."

"Pissed why?"

"I like Dr. Burr. And I know for a fact he didn't kill anyone."

"For a fact?" I raised my eyebrows.

He looked down at his shoes. "Just a figure of speech. I'm not talking hard evidence."

"Oh." I couldn't help feeling a little disappointed. "Well, come on. Why don't you get in touch with all the docs who sent us bodies from the hospital and let them know about our situation? I'll handle the murder victims."

"Okay."

He picked up a few files and trudged to the middle office like I'd asked him to take on a monumental task. I didn't really care as long as it got him out of the way so I could do a little investigating. As soon as the door closed behind him, I grabbed my phone and dashed for the cold room.

The room was pretty minimalistic; there was a long row of stainless steel cabinets and a gurney pushed against the wall with a full body bag on top. I knew who was in that bag, so I didn't even bother looking. It was the guy they'd delivered yesterday, the one I'd signed for. The bag had a big bleachy-looking stain on the side, so it was pretty distinctive.

Another clipboard hung on the wall; it took only a few seconds to figure out where Holly was stored. I opened the door to her storage unit and slid her out. This time, it was easier to look at her. Somehow, seeing her in the lab setting made it feel . . . less real, maybe. But still, I felt almost reverent as I used my cell to take pictures of the scrollwork on her face; it was a little smudged on one side, probably from the bag rubbing up against it. I photographed her clothes. Her hands were bagged, and I wasn't about to mess with that, so I contented myself with looking for any stray evidence. Coconut bits or something. But I didn't see anything. At least the damage didn't look quite as bad as it had before. Her arm was much less question-marky than I'd thought it was.

I reached out and put the tips of my fingers to her cheek. Her flesh was cold but pliant. It felt empty.

I'd seen a lot of corpses for a seventeen-year-old. Of course, some of them had gotten up and tried to eat me, but that was beside the point. Holly's body was different somehow. Sometimes I got so busy geeking out that I forgot we were talking about people. This time I couldn't forget. I looked at those ridiculous elf ears and I thought about my brother and how I would feel if he was the one stuffed into a bag in the cold room. My stomach lurched.

"Get a hold of yourself, Grable," I muttered.

I needed a breath of fresh air and maybe a good slap in the face. Sympathy was a good thing, but I told myself I could sympathize all I wanted after I got my brain in gear and put the bad guy down. Still, somehow I couldn't make myself put Holly back into that drawer, all alone in the dark. I wasn't usually the hyper-emotional type; I couldn't figure out what was wrong with me all of a sudden.

Finally, I made myself open the other storage container. This was the first murder victim, the one the police thought Dr. Burr had killed. He was young too, maybe midtwenties, with a high forehead and wide-set eyes. Something about his face looked vaguely familiar, and I stared at him for almost five minutes before I realized.

If you added a pair of elf ears and some fancy scrollwork around the eyes, he and Holly could be related. I looked back and forth between the two faces. Brother and sister, maybe? But the guy hadn't had any identification, and no one had reported a missing person yet.

I opened his bag further, searching for what had killed him. That cop had said the body was really mangled. Dr. Burr couldn't be under suspicion for both murders, since he'd been jailed when Holly was killed. If I could draw a parallel between the cases, it might clear his name. But there wasn't a single mark on the John Doe.

The door behind me opened. Just in time too. I needed a second opinion.

"Hey, Sebastian." I didn't even bother turning around. "Come take a look at this. I think maybe these two corpses are related."

He didn't say anything. I was really starting to lose my patience when I saw the look on his face. Complete horror.

"Holly?" he whimpered. "Oh, crap."

He ran out of the room. As the door swung closed behind him, I heard it. Puke makes a very distinctive sound when it splatters on floor tile.

It took me about fifteen minutes to put the bodies back after I took all my pictures, and Sebastian still hadn't come back yet. After the pukearama, he'd locked himself in the men's room across the hall. His vomit still decorated the floor in the main room; I sure hope he didn't think I was going to clean it up. That wasn't in my job description.

By then, I didn't have much time left before I had to leave to catch the bus, and I wasn't going to be late to school again. Mr. Dryer would probably force me into a life of indentured servitude in the cafeteria.

But before I left, Sebastian had some explaining to do. I found it mighty coincidental that he'd seemed to recognize the victim. Too coincidental, in fact. So I squared my shoulders, stepped over the puke, and prepared to extract the truth from him. By force, if necessary.

I tried the knob first, but the bathroom door was still locked. So I knocked.

"What?" he asked, his voice muffled.

"Are you all right?"

"Yeah, I'm okay. But I think I ate something that didn't agree with me."

"Are you sure?" I frowned. "I thought you recognized the victim."

"I think it was the Hot Pocket I had for breakfast."

"I swear you called her Holly. That's her name." There was a long pause. "Sebastian?" I prompted.

"Well, you were wrong. I said 'Holy crap.'"

"But—"

"Or maybe I did say her name. I probably read it off the chart. Now leave me alone."

Then he started making retching noises, but I was pretty sure he was acting. I would have called him on it, but I had to catch the bus. I'd beat the truth out of him later.

School, thankfully, was uneventful. I aced my Latin test and no one tried to bludgeon me with random reference materials. So I found myself walking into the basement classroom that housed our detention in a semi-good mood, which was immediately obliterated by the fact that it smelled like wet dog in there and made my allergies go haywire.

I started sneezing in the doorway and couldn't stop. When I sat down next to Kiki, she offered me a tissue.

"Thanks." I buried my nose and hoped it would help.

"You sick, Kate?" asked the pierced and studded burnout sitting next to me. "I got some Tylenol."

I couldn't decide what shocked me more: that he knew who I was or that he was talking to me like I wasn't the class brain and he wasn't carrying around enough metal to make him attractive to all magnets within a five-mile radius.

"Thanks, but it's just allergies. I think they must spray this room with Eau de Canine just to make us extra miserable."

He flashed me a grin. "Wouldn't surprise me. Let me know if you change your mind."

"Thanks again."

I got out my bio book and started to work on my homework packet, but I didn't get very far. Miss Lindsay was the detention proctor on Wednesdays, and she seemed to think that the word *proctor* was defined as "a person who stands out in the hallway, talking on her cell and not paying any attention whatsoever to what's going on in the room." The noise got so bad that after about five minutes of attempting to concentrate, I gave up.

"So what're you doing tonight?" Kiki asked, drumming a pencil on the top of her desk.

I rubbed the side of my hand. I'm a lefty, so writing in spiral notebooks hurts sometimes. "On Wednesdays, Aaron and I usually double with Rocky and Bryan."

"But not tonight?"

"I don't know. Honestly, I'm really confused. Aaron and Trey got partnered with this girl from St. Michael's, and she was throwing herself at Aaron all day yesterday. I don't like that. So I tried to hook her up with Trey, because sometimes I think he's flirting with me, and I don't like that either. But he must be sick, because he wasn't on the bus with us this morning, so now I don't know what to do."

"Wow." She blinked. "But Aaron is trustworthy. It doesn't matter how hard that girl throws herself at him."

I put my head in my hands. "So am I just overreacting? I've never had a boyfriend before. I don't know anything about relationships that isn't in the Dummies' Guide."

"Maybe a little." Kiki laughed. "I happen to know from when we dated that he hates when girls come on strong."

"Right," I said cautiously. They'd been totally over when Aaron and I got together, but I kind of hated to think of Kiki and Aaron as a couple. It gave me a serious inferiority complex.

"As for Trey . . . I don't know. He was asking about you. Like where was your locker, and about your class schedule, and stuff like that. He said he had one of your books. Did he give it to you?"

I shook my head. "I'm not missing any books."

"Well, maybe he was just fishing for info. Maybe he really is interested. He wouldn't be the first guy who fell for his best friend's girl, right?"

"Great," I muttered. "That's the last thing I need."

"It'll be okay." She patted my hand. "If he really values Aaron's friendship, he won't make any moves. All you need to do is be sensitive to his feelings."

"Sensitive. Right."

I felt about as sensitive as a Mack truck. And my nose wouldn't stop running. I honked into another tissue and tried to look confident. But the stress was getting to me. I just hoped I could hold on until the week was over without snapping.

CHAPTER
seven

Our standing double date was at my favorite diner. Its name wasn't really Legs and Eggs, but the servers all wore super-tight shirts and microscopic shorts, so we'd renamed it. It was the kind of place I normally wouldn't have set foot in except they had the best breakfast food in the known universe.

Aaron looked for a parking spot while I rushed inside. Not like I was in a huff or anything; I just needed to use the bathroom. It felt like my spleen was floating.

Rocky intercepted me at the scantily-clad-hostess station. She'd been hyperemotional lately because her boyfriend, Bryan, was getting ready to ship off to a military base in Idaho. Because really, if there was going to be an invasion, it would obviously begin in the land of the potato.

I couldn't blame her for being upset, though; I would have

felt the same way if Aaron had been about to up and leave the state. And to make matters worse, Rocky and I were both so busy that I hadn't been able to do the supportive-best-friend thing as much as I wanted.

"Hey," I said, but that was all I got out before she threw her arms around me and started sobbing on my shoulder. "What's wrong?"

"I'm so pissed!" she wailed. For once, the patrons weren't staring at the Legs or the Eggs. They were staring at us. "Bryan stood me up."

I glanced over her shoulder and saw Elle in our usual booth. She tossed her hair and gestured us over, bouncing in her seat. Great. My weekly double date was being hijacked by a Barbie-brained bimbo.

We needed privacy. I tugged Rocky toward the girls' room.

"We'll be out in a second," I said to Aaron, who'd just walked in.

He gave Rocky a sympathetic pat on the shoulder. "I'll get you a Coke."

I got Rocky some toilet paper to wipe her eyes with and persuaded her to dislodge herself long enough for me to go potty all by myself. I felt like I deserved a sticker.

When I finished, she was still sniffling and shaking. I tried to stroke her arm comfortingly with my elbow while I washed my hands. I learned quickly that the elbow has negative comfort value, but it was the thought that counted.

"So what happened?" I leaned back against the sink and held

my hands up like I was in a television medical drama. I wasn't really *that* big of a geek; public restrooms just freaked me out. When my brother was little, he used to lick the sink porcelain, and I'd had a complex ever since.

"I don't know," she said between hitching breaths.

I handed her a paper towel. She buried her nose in it and honked.

"Well, you have to know something."

"We got into a fight last night. He said . . . he wants me to go to Juilliard, and it seems silly to be together long-distance for a year and then break up because I'm going to be in New York and he's going to be in Idaho protecting the potatoes from the forces of evil."

I snorted. "Yeah, I thought the exact same thing. Really. Why Idaho?"

"But I said it was stupid to break up over something that *might* happen in the future, and as long as we're happy *now*, we should enjoy it. So he says, well, I'll think about it. He'll freaking *think* about it. And then he doesn't show up? He was supposed to be here twenty minutes ago; he won't return my calls; he's not at home. It's like he's totally avoiding me."

Now she was angry. And when Rocky got angry, she paced. This was not a problem in a gymnasium or something equally spacious. It was a big problem when you were stuffed together into a public bathroom the size of a phone booth and you had a phobia of white porcelain.

"I mean, I'm a good girlfriend, right?" she said, throwing her hands around wildly. "It's not like I'm smothering him. I just don't understand what the heck he's thinking."

"I don't get it either."

"And what's with that girl? Elle? She said Aaron invited her, and I didn't know what to think."

It took me a minute to catch up with the abrupt topic change, but then I figured she probably just wanted to get her mind off the whole Bryan thing. I couldn't blame her.

"Her dad is Aaron's mentor. And she doesn't seem to know how to take no for an answer." I shrugged. "I was pretty worked up over it, but I've got bigger things to worry about right now."

"Oh god," she said, with exaggerated fatigue. "The zombies aren't back again, are they?"

"No, it's something different." My stomach growled. "I'll tell you about it later, okay? I don't want to leave Aaron alone with the bimbo too long."

When we walked up to the booth, I nearly had a fit. Aaron was sitting next to the wall with Elle sandwiched up next to him. As I watched, she rubbed her chin against his shoulder like a cat. It kind of made me want to barf. I had two choices: I could cause a scene, or I could be the more mature person. And yeah, I knew that maturity was the right choice, especially with Aaron's mentorship at stake, but that didn't stop me from wanting to punch Elle in the nose.

While I hovered there indecisively, the waitress showed up in a pair of shorts made from about as much fabric as my left sock and a white tee plastered to her upper body. I shivered just looking at her.

My stomach rumbled, and suddenly, ordering seemed more important than teaching Elle a lesson. I sat down. Rocky launched herself into the booth next to me and ordered without even looking at the menu.

I ended up going last because I couldn't decide between the strawberry waffle and the biscuits and gravy. Then I put on my most pleasant expression and leaned forward just in time to hear Elle say, "You are such an awesomely awesome note taker, Aaron. I don't know how you do it. You're like really smart, aren't you?"

Aaron shrugged uncomfortably. "Not so much. Kate's the genius. She's much more impressive than me. Smart. Sweet. I'm lucky to have her."

I guess I didn't need to kick him after all. Our eyes met over the table, and I felt all warm and fuzzy. It would have been a really nice moment if Elle had shut her stupid yap.

"Yeah, I wish I had a smart sister," she said. "I mean, it would be so cool, because we could study together and I could borrow her notes and things like that. And it would be so much fun to have a twin. Have you guys ever pretended to be each other?"

I really hoped she was kidding, but somehow I was sure she wasn't. I wanted to laugh, or maybe shake her head really hard to see if it rattled. But I contented myself with smirking in Rocky's direction. Unfortunately, she was way too engrossed in her iPhone to notice. Texting Bryan, probably.

The amusement faded pretty fast, mostly because Elle put her head on Aaron's shoulder. He looked at me with a panicked expression, and I was so done. I understood his ambition. Heck, I shared it. And if that meant he felt like his hands were tied with regard to putting Elle in her place, I'd just have to be the bad guy.

"I don't think you get it." I crossed my arms and glared at her. "Aaron is my boyfriend."

"Yeah, right." She laughed so hard she snorted.

This got Rocky's attention; she slammed her hand on the table so hard that the silverware rattled. "Not a joke!"

Our waitress picked that moment to return with those stupid shorts barely covering her butt, a tray full of food, and a concerned look on her face. Elle stalked off toward the bathrooms and boy, was I going to miss her. I asked the waitress to box up her stupid salad plate.

"Is she okay?" asked the waitress.

"Oh yeah." I nodded reassuringly. "She's got cephaloproctitis and she forgot her medicine. That's all."

Her eyes widened as she placed my plate of greasy-spoon goodness on the table. After she left, Rocky said, "Cephalopro-whatsis?"

"*Cephalo* means 'head' and *proctitis* means 'up the butt.' Essentially."

Aaron laughed so hard that he choked. And the world was right again.

I'd like to say everything went smoothly after that, but it didn't. Elle returned to the table more obnoxious than ever. Throughout the rest of dinner, she went so overboard with the hair toss-ing and back arching that I would have said she had Tourette's if I didn't know better. After she threw a fit about the to-go box, she kept trying to feed Aaron bits from it despite the fact that cottage cheese made him break out in hives. And she let out this hyena laugh every time he said something, even if it wasn't remotely funny.

The check couldn't come quickly enough. I stood up about a half second after the waitress took our money. I couldn't wait to get rid of Elle so I could tell Rocky and Aaron all about the mur-der. In all the relationship-related excitement, I was embarrassed to admit that I'd totally forgotten.

But Elle wasn't as eager to go home as I was. "Hey, hand-some?" she cooed to Aaron. "Can you give me a ride home?"

CHAPTER eight

Elle yapped all the way out to the Legs and Eggs parking lot, and my earmuffs did nothing to stifle the noise. The walk outside only took two minutes, but it felt like an eternity.

"My parents will flip if I don't get home soon," she said, sticking her lower lip out so far that I wanted to get a stapler and fasten that puppy back in place. "And my car is in the shop. I mean, how hard is it to fix a tire rim? So annoying."

"No prob," Aaron said. "Friends don't abandon each other in parking lots. I'll take you home. Kate, do you want to come?"

"Where do you live?" I asked Elle.

She looked down her nose at me. "Ottawa Pointe."

Crap. Ottawa Pointe was almost a half hour away. I couldn't handle thirty minutes more of Elle. Not without earplugs. Or tranquilizers. And I was determined not to let her get to me. She wasn't going to make me into the jealous girlfriend, no matter how hard she tried.

"Nah. I think I'll go with Rocky."

"Are you sure?" he asked. "I was hoping we could hang out later."

"You could drop her off and come over afterward. If you want?"

"I'd like that," he said.

He cupped my cheek in one hand and kissed me. It was a relatively chaste, public kind of kiss, but my knees still went a little shaky. Aaron had that effect on me, even after all this time.

And as an added bonus, it made Elle all red-faced and furious.

They left. It took two steps before Elle plastered herself to Aaron's side. He tried to dodge her, but she was persistent. By the time they'd made it to his car, they were practically sharing his jeans. If this kept up much longer, she would have to start paying rent. If I didn't kill her first.

Rocky elbowed me in the side. "You should have gone with them."

I watched them drive off, Elle babbling like an idiot while Aaron stared stone-faced at the road.

"Believe me, it was tempting. But if I can't trust my boyfriend, we shouldn't be dating, right?"

"You're a much better person than me," she said. "I spent most of that meal trying to figure out where to kick Bryan first. I was going to go with the testicles, but that's so cliché, don't you think?"

I was about to reply when a long, drawn-out howl split the air. My head turned to follow the sound; it had come from somewhere behind the building.

"What was that?" Rocky huddled close to me like I might offer some protection.

"A dog or a wolf, maybe?" I rubbed my arms; they'd erupted into gooseflesh. "The only way I can tell for sure is if I get close enough to start sneezing. Unless it's one of those hypoallergenic dogs like Armstrong, in which case I'm no help whatsoever."

"Funny. So you want to get going?"

"Sure."

But I found myself dragging my feet on the way to her car. Something seemed off, a niggling feeling that I couldn't shake. The parking lot was overflowing with minivans and sedans. Somebody had parked an SUV illegally in the handicapped spot, but I was pretty sure that wasn't what was bothering me. I couldn't see anybody, and when I smelled the air, all I got was the cold tang of impending snow.

"What's up?" asked Rocky.

"I dunno," I whispered. "Shhh."

I stuffed my freezing hands in the pockets of my coat and wandered out into the middle of the parking lot, trying to figure out what had me so spooked. It felt like my whole body was one big goose bump now, and my hands were shaking with adrenaline. I'd learned to trust those instincts before. The worst thing that could happen was that I'd look dumb, right?

Then I saw a dark splatter on the ground near a white SUV

parked at the back end of the lot near the Dumpsters. Normally, random muck didn't exactly command my attention, but this did. The dark liquid glinted in the dim light.

I didn't need to touch it to figure out what it was. As soon as I got close, I could smell the blood. There was another smear on the back of a pickup. Apparently, my poor eyesight didn't apply to bloodstains, or maybe the adrenaline rush had enhanced my visual acuity.

Something in the overgrown lot behind the restaurant clanged loudly.

"Meet me around back!" I yelled, pointing to the right. "We'll cut it off."

Rocky took off like this was an Olympic trial. I hiked my backpack more securely onto my shoulders and circled the building to the left. We'd catch whatever was back there. And do something constructive with it that I hadn't thought of yet.

Being a total med geek had its advantages. My pack was stuffed with medical paraphernalia just in case I happened to run across a random emergency.

"Is someone hurt?" I yelled. It came out as more of a gasp than a yell—I wasn't exactly a track star. It didn't surprise me when no one answered. I knew from the amount of blood on the ground that this was a serious injury. The victim most likely was unconscious. You don't spot bloodstains from a skinned knee at a hundred meters. If you do, you're a freak. I was a geek; that was totally different.

I stopped at the chain-link fence bordering the back of the

lot. The lot was crammed with junk—snow-speckled boxes and empty pallets competed for space with beer cans and random bits of broken furniture. To make matters worse, it was much more difficult to see back here. The roof of the restaurant blocked all the lights, and we were in that gray borderland between dusk and full night.

The pavement crunched beneath my shoes as I twisted on the balls of my feet, searching for some sound or smell that would lead me to the person—or thing—that was bleeding. Nothing.

There was another thunderous clatter from the far end of the lot. It sounded like someone skydiving onto a trash can. But I still couldn't see anything. The lot was so overgrown that you could have hidden a freaking tank in there and no one would have noticed.

To go around the fence would waste precious seconds. I sprinted right up the back of a pickup truck parked next to it, setting off the alarm. The monotonous *wah-wah* noise made my teeth vibrate. Good; maybe it would attract some assistance. Something told me I was going to need it.

I climbed onto the cab and vaulted the fence before I had a chance to rethink. The fence wasn't particularly high, but anything requiring physical skill made me nervous by default. My ankle twisted a little on the landing, but otherwise, the Jumping Off Random Objects fairies were looking out for me. I started puffing like an asthmatic in a balloon factory, but I ran on, my head whipping from side to side, looking for blood spatter in the piles of cast-off bottles and half-rotten pallets.

Finally, I saw it. All the way at the back of the lot was a slowly rolling trash can, and then I could make out a crumpled form against the chain-link fence. The ground shimmered; someone lay sprawled there in a big black pool of goop. It could only be blood, and my heart sank when I saw how much there was.

That was nothing compared to how I felt when I saw that the victim was Rocky's boyfriend, Bryan.

Rocky ran through the gate with my backpack slung over her shoulder. She'd be here in seconds. I didn't want her to see him like this, but I couldn't save him alone.

"I need you to stay calm," I called over to her. She stopped a few feet away, a look of horror on her face. Even in the dim light, even with his face turned away, she knew. "You deserve to fall apart right now, but I need you to help me. Can you do it?"

The gravel piffed as she flung the backpack in my direction. "I'll call 911." Her voice wobbled, but she whipped out her cell and started dialing. I'd just have to trust that she could tell them what they needed to know.

I turned back to Bryan. There was just enough light left for me to see. I needed to staunch the blood flow, although by the size of this pool, I knew it was probably too late. He'd be lucky if he escaped this without brain damage. Heck, he'd be lucky if he didn't die.

There was so much blood. I tore open a thick gauze pad to staunch the wound. But I couldn't find one.

I sat back on my heels for a second; that was how shocked I

was. Maybe the blood wasn't his? But if that was true, why was he unconscious?

Idiot. I smacked myself on the forehead; I couldn't afford to sit here theorizing while there could be internal damage. I leaned over to check his respiration. His chest shuddered in a pained, almost convulsive movement.

Something wasn't right. I flipped my hair over my shoulder and put my ear to his mouth but didn't hear any air going in. And now that I knew what to look for, I could see the red splotches slowly surfacing on his neck under the streaks of blood. Purpura. Normally, the opportunity to see some purpura up close and personal would make me go all geeky, but right now it just made me want to throw up, because I knew what it meant.

His windpipe was smashed.

I fumbled for the backpack. He didn't have much time before he suffocated; I needed gloves and I needed them now. But my hands were shaking so hard that I couldn't open the zipper. Too bad Elle wasn't here. I bet she was an expert at unzipping things.

Screw it. I put my bare hands on his gore-smeared face, even though I knew I was exposing myself to a big pool of potential infection. I refused to let Bryan die because I was too busy worrying about myself. Then I gently levered his jaw forward even though I knew, I just knew it wasn't going to open the airway. But I needed to try everything before I cut him.

Rocky fell to her knees beside me. "The ambulance will be here in a few," she said. "Oh my god, Bryan?" She shook his shoulder, tears dripping off the end of her nose. "Baby, can you hear me?"

"He's suffocating," I said. "Open my bag."

Tactless, I knew, but I was focused on the fact that I was about to perform minor surgery on one of my friends in the middle of a dimly lit, junk-strewn gravel lot. It didn't even register that I'd stuck my foot in it until I realized she wasn't moving. She just sat there with her mouth hanging open, staring at Bryan like he might miraculously heal himself.

So I shook her, just hard enough to get her attention. My hands left bloody prints on her shoulders, and she peeped indignantly. Literally peeped.

I choked back hysterical laughter. "Dump the bag. I'm going to open an airway; you've got to hand me the right equipment. Please, Rocky. I need you to believe in me, because I'm scared shitless."

She took in a shuddering breath. "Okay. What am I looking for?"

"Alcohol wipes, the pink scalpel case, and a pen. Ballpoint, not Sharpie."

She upended the pack onto the ground. Good. I turned back to Bryan. It looked like I was going to get to do a little surgery this week after all. Funny how things worked out.

Rocky shoved the pen at me with one hand, still raking through the scattered mess with the other. I pulled it apart, removing the ink cartridge. Then I tilted Bryan's head back and put the extra gauze underneath his neck to brace it.

His neck was so lumpy that it took me a minute to figure out which lump was the Adam's apple. I hoped I was doing this right;

I'd practiced this procedure on my Cabbage Patch Kids, but it wasn't exactly the same.

I tore open a scalpel. It would have felt so cool if it hadn't been for the fact that my hand was shaking like I was a crackhead with a tremor. And when it was time to make the incision, I froze. I was a high school student, for god's sake. I didn't care how big a med geek I was; I should not have been doing makeshift surgery on my best friend's boyfriend. If I killed him, I would never be able to face Rocky again.

But he'd die if I did nothing.

That did it. I made the cut decisively, forcing my hands to remain steady. Then I wormed the pen tube into his neck. There wasn't much resistance; this whole process was a lot easier than I'd expected. Of course, I'd probably jinxed myself by thinking that. I said a quick prayer and puffed into the exposed end of the pen. His chest rose and fell as the air filled his lungs. Hallelujah.

I settled down next to him on my knees, the end of my braid skimming the pool of blood on his face. It was twenty kinds of gross, but I would have hated myself if I'd let worry about my stupid hair get in the way of my job, and my hands were so gory that I'd only make it worse if I tried to pull my braid out of the way.

Between puffs, I asked for some gauze. Rocky stared at me like I was speaking Swahili. Frankly, I was surprised she'd held together as long as she had. I groped around for the gauze myself.

The stupid car alarm was still going off, but no one came to investigate. I thought someone ought to make a car alarm that repeatedly shouted, "Free beer!" I bet loads of people would come for that.

I mopped the blood off Bryan's face with one hand, held the pen steady with the other, and periodically breathed into it until he started respirating on his own again.

I felt like a total rock star.

CHAPTER
nine

The EMTs arrived after what felt like an eternity. The ambulance was too wide to fit through the gate, so they had to park at Legs and Eggs. If I'd been in charge, I would have driven monster truck–style right over the stupid fence, but I obviously had different priorities than most of the world's population.

Besides, I couldn't complain. Bryan seemed stable; Rocky was content to hold his hand and repeatedly brush the hair from his forehead, and the slight delay gave me a little time to investigate. I was more determined than ever to find the person or thing that had done this. And then I'd kick its butt.

I kept a steady grip on the pen so it didn't go all wonky on me while I looked around for evidence. Bryan had a bloody knife gripped in his hand; I nearly stabbed myself in the thigh when I leaned over him. I made a mental note to search the attack victim for pointy objects the next time something like this happened.

He must have done some serious damage with that knife if the blood pool was any indication. I had no idea how the bad guy could have gotten over the fence after sustaining such a massive injury, but it didn't matter how far he ran. He wasn't getting away from me, damn it. He should have known better than to mess with the science geek.

I groped around in the scattered med supplies for a spare specimen vial. I'd started carrying them around with me after the almost-zombocalypse. EDTA tubes would have been handy, because they keep blood from clotting, but there was geekery and then there was obsessive-compulsive straitjacket territory. A dangerous line, but I toed it well.

A quick flick of my thumb and the vial popped open. I let the knife drip into it. A clump of something wiry stuck on the edge of the vial. When I tried to remove it, it stuck to the side of my red-streaked finger. Great.

The EMTs shoved their gurney onto the gravel; it bounced and rattled over the uneven ground, but they were still closing in on us fast. I needed to hide my samples pronto, or I'd lose them. For some reason, medical professionals get all crazy about high school students taking medical samples from a crime scene.

I squinted at the wiry stuff in the dim light. It was hair. Lots of hair. Little clumps of it were scattered around the blood pool. Bryan had a bunch in his hand. There was no way it was his; he had a buzz cut. So it had to be from his attacker. My overactive imagination treated me to a great visual of Bryan, stabbing wildly with the knife as his attacker throttled him, blood and hair spattering down on his face. Ick. I had to concentrate on the positives.

That hair was like trace evidence from the gods.

I'd probably just saved Bryan's life, so the cops wouldn't begrudge me a sample of that too. Or at least, they wouldn't if I didn't tell them I took it.

Out came another vial, and I shoved a few strands of hair into it. When I stuffed the samples in my pocket, my hand left a streak of gore down the front of my favorite jeans. The things I sacrificed in the name of medicine.

The two EMTs finally made it over to us, dashing over and evaluating Bryan at lightning speed. One of them, an older guy with about three strands of hair left, looked up and said, "Which one of you is Kate?"

I raised a freezing, red streaked hand. "That would be me."

"Don't go anywhere. We need to talk to you once we're done."

He was looking at me like I'd done something wrong, and that kind of ticked me off. What did a girl have to do to earn a thank-you around here? Save the world?

Oh, wait. I'd already done that.

"Fine," I huffed. "But I'm going inside to wash my hands first."

I didn't wait for permission. I stalked back into the restaurant with my gory hands held up in front of my face. The hostess took one look at me and shrieked at the top of her lungs.

"Quit screaming and open the bathroom door for me," I said.

"I just conducted impromptu surgery in your back lot, and I don't want to drip on your floor."

My matter-of-fact tone snapped her out of it.

"Ohmigod," she said. "Of course. Right this way, Miss Grable."

Some guy in a corner booth took out his cell and snapped a picture. It was so tempting to flip him off, but I reminded myself that I wasn't mad at him. I was mad at the hairball who'd nearly killed one of my friends.

The hostess opened the bathroom door for me and turned on the hot water. After I scalded my hands for about ten minutes, they finally started to warm up. I'd been really lucky that we were in a relatively warm snap and the temperature hadn't dipped below freezing. Blood gets really cold after it's been drying on your hands for about a half hour.

In the time it took me to scrub the blood out from under my fingernails, the entire waitstaff had congregated outside the bathroom, and they pounced as soon as I opened the door. Anyone close enough to touch me did—they patted my shoulder and shook my hand and thanked whatever deity happened to be listening that I'd been in the right place at the right time. Someone started applauding, and the noise quickly spread through the restaurant. I endured it with flaming cheeks and attempted to teleport somewhere else. Anywhere that didn't have tons of people simultaneously trying to climb into my lap. It didn't work.

"Here," said our waitress from earlier, wrapping her arm around me and thrusting a to-go cup in my hands. "Black coffee, extra strong. Just the way you like it."

"Thanks. Would it be too much trouble to get another one for my friend? Her boyfriend is the one who got attacked."

"You hold on for a second."

That was how I found myself treating the entire crew of assorted civil servants to coffee and fresh pastries. I walked back outside trailed by a little parade of girls, winter coats pulled on over their skimpy outfits, bearing hot food. One of the EMTs nearly swallowed his tongue when he saw us coming.

I thanked the Leg and Eggers again and made a beeline for Rocky with a hot cup of caffeinated goodness. "Thanks," she said, huddling over the steam but not once removing her eyes from Bryan's face. He was already strapped onto the stretcher. I'd give these guys one thing—they worked fast.

"We're heading out now, miss," the near-tongue-swallower said to Rocky. "Did you get in touch with his mother?"

"Yeah. She's on her way to the hospital now."

"Good." He patted her on the shoulder. "I know the cops want to talk to you, but you come on over once you've cleared things up with them. He's gonna be okay."

She rubbed her red-rimmed eyes. "Thanks."

I hugged her then, and she'd just started to cry it out when those tactless idiot police decided this was an ideal time to start interrogating us. They split us up and made us stand out there in the cold for almost an hour. I told the story about how we found Bryan. The cops made me go through it twice because they thought it might jog my memory. And then Despain showed up, and I told her too.

"I've got to tell you, girlie," she said, briskly rubbing her glove-less hands together, "it's awfully coincidental that you keep show-ing up at these attacks."

Oh my god. She thought I was a murderer. Maybe she sensed my residual guilt over the samples; I wanted to confess that I'd taken them. And one time they accidentally gave me two ham-burgers at McDonald's, and I didn't go back to pay for the extra one. I felt like I should spill it all just to make her stop looking at me like that.

"Are you sure there's nothing you're not telling me?" she asked, looking at me closely.

I shook my head vigorously. "No, ma'am. I'm just a magnet for weird stuff. That's all. Actually, that's a lie; I'm also a closet stalker of medical professionals."

I sounded like a wackjob. Frankly, I was resigned to wackjob city. I was pretty much a permanent resident by this point.

Despain grinned. "Tell me something I don't know. Listen, I'll be in touch once I know more. If you figure something out, you call me. Understand? No going off on your own to save the day again. I'll believe whatever you've got to say, no matter how weird. Deal?"

"Deal."

She walked away, and then Rocky practically knocked me over. I assumed it was supposed to be a hug, but it felt more like a tackle. I barely managed to maintain my balance. Of course, I was highly motivated, since we'd be toppling over into the pool of blood if we fell.

"Thank you, Kate. You're a life saver." Her damp cheek pressed against mine.

"It's what I'm here for," I said, but my face still flushed with the praise. "Have you heard anything about Bryan yet?"

"They said he's going to be okay, thanks to you."

If she didn't stop complimenting me soon, my head would explode. With all the gore around here, probably no one would notice.

"Are you ready to go?" she asked.

"Rocky, I can find a ride. I bet Despain would take me home once she's done here. Go see Bryan."

"I'm driving you home so you can figure out who did this." She grabbed my arms and hissed, keeping her voice low so the cops didn't hear. "You find the bastard and nail his testes to the wall, you hear me?"

I pulled the vials out of my pocket, hunching over them so no one would see. "I intend to. And I'm hoping these will help me do it."

"Good."

Our eyes met. She looked as mad as I felt.

At home, I stopped by the study to tell my dad why I was late. He was watching something on SyFy; from his surprised expression, my lateness hadn't even registered. Probably because he'd been watching TV with his eyes closed again.

I fortified myself with caffeine and then went downstairs. Our basement was Geek Central. The stairs opened right into Jonah's domain; it was dominated by a large computer desk strewn with random electronic thingies and empty Mountain Dew cans. The rest of the floor space was covered in foam mats so he and his friends could pretend to be elven gladiators without hurting themselves.

The people who'd owned our house before us had had a bedroom in the basement, and I'd converted it into a lab. After I'd neutralized the zombie infestation, the school gave me all my chemistry teacher's old lab equipment. They didn't have the space to store it or the know-how to use it, and she was serving jail time, so she didn't exactly need it either. So the former bedroom was stuffed with lab geekery: a microscope, a centrifuge, a lab bench, and even a fume hood, although I couldn't figure out how to hook up the ventilation, so that was pretty much for show.

Jonah stood in the middle of the mats, waving around a sword covered in pink foam. My brother's brand of geekery had become increasingly popular since we'd fought off the zombies with his pseudoswords. The swords were really just PVC pipe wrapped with foam and duct tape, but he was delusional enough to insist that we refer to them as swords.

Jonah's moves weren't that bad; he actually managed a halfway decent spin kick as I came into the room. But I still had to suppress a snort. What could I say? Elf ears, frilly tunics, and bright orange leggings cracked me up.

The three geek girls sitting against the wall didn't seem to mind, though. Beneath their ridiculous face paint and stupid costumes, they watched him with expressions of total adoration.

I had to concede one thing to Jonah; he'd always claimed magic was possible. After witnessing his newfound popularity with the ladies, I couldn't argue with him anymore.

When he saw the samples in my hands and the bloodstains on my clothes, he stopped midspin and nearly chopped his own head off. Or he would have, if decapitation by pseudosword had been possible. The geek girls didn't seem to notice. They ooohed appreciatively.

"Is it the zombies again?" Jonah's voice contained much more eagerness than the question really deserved.

"Nope." I pushed past him en route to my lab. His groupies shrank back from me with reverence. If my friend hadn't just been mauled, I might have felt pretty flattered.

"Something new?" he said. "Is it vampires? Staking vampires would be so awesome!"

He tugged repeatedly on my shoulder. If I didn't tell him something, he'd bring his whole PVC-infested crew into my lab. My lab was not PVC compatible. My mental health wasn't either; at least not today.

"Maybe. I don't know."

As far as answers go, this one was about as generic as they came, and it had completely unexpected results. Jonah started barking out orders like a drill sergeant; he sounded pretty impressive except for the part where his voice kept cracking.

"You heard her, girls!" he barked. The girls leapt to their feet, teeth bared and mock swords held in white-knuckled hands.

They didn't look intimidating; they looked terrified. "Plan Alpha. Starfire, call the troops and put them on high alert. Europa and Calamity, establish a perimeter around the house. Kate, what's our target?"

"Target?" I blinked. He was kind of freaking me out right now. And I was trying to figure out which one of these washrag-looking girls thought Calamity was a good choice for a nickname. Because I thought someone should tell her she was delusional.

"Target. As in what kind of creature are we defending you from?"

"Oh. Um ... it's something really hairy. And strong. Possibly with claws. I don't know if we're talking animal or human yet."

"Hairy?" He was so excited that he practically vibrated. "Do you realize what this means? *Werewolf awesomeness!*"

The girls all started squealing. I realized at that moment that I would never understand people at all. Although this was probably not a representative sample.

"Don't be ridiculous," I scoffed. "There are plenty of other potential explanations."

"Like what?"

"Um ... well." I couldn't come up with any other explanations, damn it. "Well, maybe it's a really strong guy with long fingernails and a severe case of hypertrichosis."

"Hyper-whatsis?"

"Excessive body hair."

He snorted at me. The gall.

"It's better than the werewolf theory," I snapped. "I'd probably be able to come up with a better explanation if you'd let me get into my damned lab!"

He backed out of my way but didn't look apologetic. And when I stomped into my lab, he followed me. At least the geek-eteers didn't come too. They shouldered their PVC and scrambled off to their battle stations.

I went into the bathroom and washed my hands with the speed of a Marvel superhero. I didn't want to give Jonah enough unsupervised time to break anything. When I came back out, he was squinting at the specimen vials, trying to figure out what was inside. He took one look at me and dropped them on the floor in an attempt to look innocent.

"You dork," I said, but it didn't have much heat to it. If I'd been left alone in a room with some mystery samples, I would have checked them out too.

"Sorry."

He shouldered his sword and moved out of my way. I ignored him as best I could, pulling out a box full of slide-related paraphernalia. Rocky had a secret stash of chocolate. Jonah had some very embarrassing magazines that I found under his bed the one time he stole my glasses and refused to give them back. And then there was me. I hoarded boxes of slides, because I was twenty different kinds of pitiful.

I wormed my hands into a pair of gloves and started assembling the slides. I was just preparing a piece of wet-mounted perfection when the hairs stood up on the back of my neck. Someone was watching me. I looked up, half expecting to see a huge, hairy serial crusher, but it was only my brother. It was nice to have a personal guard and all, but something told me his technique of staring at me gape-mouthed wasn't really going to dissuade any potential intruders.

The distraction made me place the cover slip crooked. Now my slide was smeared. In my lab, a smeary slide pretty much signifies that the apocalypse is coming. It just isn't done.

"Jonah," I said. "If you don't stop hanging over my shoulder, I will infect you with elephantiasis."

"Not possible." He shuffled from foot to foot, thinking it through. "Is it?"

"It's a parasite; of course it's possible. You'll be lugging your testicles around in a wheelbarrow if you don't leave me alone."

"Gross," he said, with an admiring nod. He managed to stay quiet for about fifteen seconds. "Can't I do something to help?"

"You are helping," I muttered, trying to keep my arm steady as I administered just the right amount of pressure to my saline dropper. "You and your girlfriends are protecting me from whatever-this-is."

"Look, we both know that's utter bull. It's just a good way to keep the girls from messing with your lab. I know how much you hate that."

"Thanks."

This time, the cover slip slid into position without a single jiggle. Not an air bubble in sight.

When I turned around, Jonah's face smacked into my

shoulder. I was so glad he wasn't about a half a foot shorter, because then he would have hit my chest, and that would have been made of awkward.

"Would you back off?" I snarled.

I had to get him off my back before we had another murder on our hands. Because really, he was about an inch away from death by pipette.

"So have you learned anything about Holly?" I asked. "Or do you know anybody you can ask? I need to know if she has a brother. I think he might be in my morgue."

He tapped his chin thoughtfully. "I can ask around. Most people don't give out identifying info online, but I bet somebody would know. Calamity was saying that she thought Holly's boyfriend also played *Dragons of Roargan Kross*. Maybe I could hunt him down."

"Do it. I'll take any info you can get on her. Or the boyfriend. And leave me alone before I infect you with elephantiasis."

"You have elephantiasis on the brain."

"But not elephantiasis of the brain."

He grinned at me before going out to boot up his computer. I was alone in my lab again. It made me so happy I could have squeed.

CHAPTER

ten

The lab work was easy, but my results didn't make sense. And we're not talking Nobel-level science here. There's a simple rhythm to making a wet-mount slide. Pick a blank slide. Apply the saline. Scrape some sample from the pellet. Apply the sample to the slide. I had no idea how I could have messed it up, but stranger things had happened. I'd witnessed a lot of them.

I'd just have to start all over. I began pulling out the necessary equipment a little more aggressively than I probably should have, but I was ticked. A box of slides fell to the floor with a clatter and the tinkle of broken glass. I said a very bad word. Twice. Loudly, even.

As I stood there surveying the mess, my cell beeped. I was tempted to ignore it, but I couldn't, not under the circumstances. I thought it might be Rocky, but wrong again. It was Aaron.

Not too late to come over, is it?

It took me forever to type a reply. I was über-paranoid about sounding like the desperate girlfriend. After about three tries at political correctness, I just gave up and typed what I was thinking.

Dad's downstairs, and it's after curfew. Maybe I can sneak outside?

His reply came within seconds: Meet me on your roof.

I had to read it twice. Evidently, my boyfriend had hidden reservoirs of insanity, because my roof wasn't tops on my list of places to hang out. Yes, my dormer window opened right onto the shingles, and yes, Aaron had helped us clean out the gutters a little over a month ago. And yes, he'd made some comment about meeting up there sometime to stargaze, but I hadn't taken it seriously. Apparently, I'd been wrong.

Well, I wasn't about to argue, particularly since he'd just spent a long time in the car with Elle. I didn't realize how long until I glanced up at the clock midway through washing my hands. He'd been gone for two hours. I'd lost track of the time in the lab. And the shower. During my brief bathroom break, I'd used up enough hot water to melt the Arctic Circle.

It didn't take a math whiz to figure out something didn't add up. A half hour to Ottawa Pointe. Five minutes to drop Elle off, assuming he didn't just slow down and shove her out the window, which was what I would have done. A half hour back. Even if he'd gone five miles under the speed limit, even if he'd stopped to go to the bathroom, there was no reason it should have taken two freaking hours to drop her off.

I threw on a hoodie and stomped up the stairs, fully intending to catapult my boyfriend off the top of the house. When I climbed out the window, my socks caught on the rough surface of the shingles. The fact that I'd forgotten to put shoes on only made me angrier. All I'd wanted was to be in the Future Doctors of America program. I'd been looking forward to it for months. And now where was I? FDA mentor accused of murder. Friend in the hospital. Boyfriend developing crappy tendencies. And nothing to show for all my lab work but a pile of broken glass.

So when Aaron climbed up the trellis, I let him have it.

"Why weren't you back sooner?" I demanded, practically spitting the words in his face.

He completely ignored me. Instead, he hoisted himself up onto the roof one-handed and gave me my second giant to-go cup of the night, hot to the touch. Then he reached into his shirt and pulled out a white paper bag.

"Lucky I didn't spill it on the way up," he said. "I asked them to brew you a fresh cup, because the first one they gave me tasted like something died in it. And then on the way out of the Grabbit Quik, I ran into my neighbor, and she wouldn't stop talking about her new Pomeranian."

I felt instantly, terribly guilty. I tried to stammer out an apology, but he rode right over me. I wasn't sure if he didn't notice my wenchiness, or he was just kindly giving me a way to extract my foot from my mouth with some semblance of grace.

"There's a muffin in there too, if you're hungry," he said.

The muffin was almost too much to take. I settled myself precariously on the slanted roof, sipped my coffee, and debated trying to kick myself in the butt. I wasn't sure it was possible to get a good quality self-butt-kick, and I really didn't think I should try it two stories off the ground. Not with Aaron here to watch me fall. I didn't have much of a chance of keeping him as it was, not with my amazing twin powers of idiocy and jealousy.

Maybe I should call it jidiocy.

All this ran through my head while I drank my coffee and Aaron played with the end of my braid. I knew I should say something witty and alluring, or throw myself into his lap and make him forget all about Elle. But I'd had way too much to process today. Too much death, even for a med geek like me.

"You okay?" he asked. "No offense, but you're acting kind of strange."

It would have been too easy to take offense, but I was tired of being a drama queen. So I told him everything. I tried to stick to the facts, but I still got a little emotional. In retrospect, so many things could have gone wrong, and that above everything else scared the bleep out of me.

"Wow," he said when I was done. "So what now?"

"Well, I came home to analyze the hair and blood, right? I'm not set up to sequence DNA, and I wouldn't have anything to compare it to anyway, so I know I can't ID the culprit, but at least I could give us something to go on. Knowing the attacker is a Caucasian male is better than nothing, right?"

"Makes sense to me."

"But I can't even prove that." My words came out clipped and whiny. I was a genius, right? I should have at least been able to generate data that made sense. "I've got to do the analysis all over again."

"Why?"

"Well, unless you know somebody with mutant hair, freakish strength, and magnetic blood, I think I got something wrong."

"Mutant—what?" He ran his hands through his hair the way he did when he was thinking hard. I barely restrained myself from stripping down to my underwear right there; it was just that sexy. But I was wearing my Sci FIVE! underwear. Sci five: like a high five, only geekier. Because sure, I was a reformed geek on the outside, but inside? I really hadn't changed, and I had no intention of doing so. This plan sat pretty well with me except at times like now when I realized that geekdom and sex appeal don't exactly go well together.

"Tell me about it," I said, pulling my mind out of the gutter. "I must have made some mistake. Because the hair isn't human. And I discovered that the blood has metal in it, because the pellet got stuck to my desk magnet. So either I contaminated it, or . . ."

"It's probably a werewolf. Or maybe a magnetic Yeti."

"Har har. You're so funny."

"Not kidding, Kate. It's the only theory that really explains your findings. Mutant hair. Funky blood. The most logical explanation is that you're looking for something not entirely human."

"Yeah, but even if that weren't completely rat-in-a-coffee-can insane, it still doesn't explain the metal."

"Maybe he overdosed on red meat? Lots of iron? It seems like a werewolfy thing to do."

"I don't believe in werewolves," I said emphatically. "Or Yeti either. And I only believe in viral zombies, not voodoo ones. I'm looking for scientifically probable explanations, not wackjob conspiracy theories."

My brother opened his window and stuck his head out, grinning like an idiot. "Did someone say werewolf?"

I attempted to snort at him derisively, because it was so like Jonah to get all worked up about some gamer-geek thing when we had a medical mystery to solve. Unfortunately, I forgot to swallow the coffee first. It shot right up into my sinuses, scorching my nose hairs and nearly causing my eyeballs to fly out of their sockets.

So then I did the choking and coughing thing. It got even more blazingly attractive when Jonah handed me a tissue through the open window and I horked caffeinated snot all over it.

"You okay?" asked Aaron.

"I'll survive," I replied, even though I still wasn't entirely sure.

"So do you really think it could be one?" Jonah climbed out the window and slid halfway off the roof before he managed to stop himself. Nearly gave me a freaking heart attack. "A werewolf, I mean?"

"Don't fall off, you idiot," I croaked. "And I thought you were supposed to be doing research on our victim, not daydreaming about lupine shape-shifters. This is serious, Jonah."

"I know. And I've got some intel for you."

"Then what are you dorking around for? Spill it," I ordered.

"Is Aaron up to speed here?" he asked. Aaron nodded. It kind of surprised me that they got along so well, but they had pretty much saved each other's lives, so I guess they were inclined to like each other. Besides, they didn't hang out much. Jonah was great in small doses.

"So let's see," he said. "I ran into a couple of members of the Clan of Awesome online tonight. Actually, I didn't run into them per se; one of my tanks knows a healer from C of A. They've cosplayed together a couple of times. It's all just a matter of cultivating connections, you know."

"Cos-what?" I asked.

"Cosplay. Dressing up in costumes like—"

"I don't want to know." I sighed. "Get to the point."

The geek speak hurt my brain, and massaging my temples didn't seem to help. Aaron slipped an arm around my waist and pulled me close, which only served to agitate me further. I mean, it was nice, but it wasn't exactly calming.

"You are so impatient." Jonah shook a finger at me but had the good sense to stop when I glared at him. "All right. Holly had a twin brother named—get this—Herbie. He went to school somewhere else. I also found out that she was a waitress, lived on her own, and was getting her nursing degree at the community college. She spent most of her spare time playing *Roargan Kross*. The only person in the Clan of Awesome who met her IRL was her boyfriend."

"IRL?" said Aaron.

"In real life." Jonah flipped through a sheaf of scribbled notes. "The boyfriend played a Wyvern half-breed wizard with spiky blue hair and a leather trench, if that tells you anything."

"It doesn't," I said. "You don't happen to know anything useful about him, do you? I can't exactly tell the cops to put out an APB on a Wyvern whatever."

"His character's name was Lucern. My contact didn't know his real name, but I've got some feelers out."

"All right." I took a deep breath and let it out slow. So someone had killed Holly and her brother. Had they seen something? If so, why hadn't she gone to the police after he'd come up missing? And why hadn't their parents reported it? I had plenty of data, but I couldn't put it together in a way that made sense. "Thanks," I added belatedly.

"Lunatic gamer werewolves," Jonah said. "If that's not the coolest thing ever, I don't know what is." He practically vibrated with excitement. I was beginning to think my brother had a secret lupine fetish. It frightened me.

"I'm still not convinced," I replied.

"Dude, don't you listen to yourself? If you put your huge hairy guy together with your rabid animal, you get a werewolf. Didn't you see the Twilight movies?" He put a fist on his hip and wagged his finger at us. The sight scarred me; I squeezed my eyes shut and wished for a self-lobotomizer. It didn't work.

"No," Aaron said. "I did not. And I'm proud of that."

"Well," my brother said, "you should. It's the only explanation that makes sense."

"It doesn't make sense," I snapped. "We're trying for scientifically feasible explanations, Jonah. Not some stupid fairy tale."

Jonah put his other fist on his hip and started sliding off the roof again. He grabbed his window and held on tight. "Excuse me. You're the one who cured the zombie virus. Maybe you should think about that before you write me off."

"Excuse *me*." I was about to really tear into him when Aaron scooted between us and held up his hands. I immediately backed off, only not physically because I would have toppled over the gutters. I bet Elle didn't pick infantile fights with her brother. She was probably too busy gallivanting around her house in teeny cami pajamas right now, making plans to steal my boyfriend. My only consolation was that if there really was a serial killer on the loose, she'd be one of the first to go. The girls in teeny camis never make it.

"I think," Aaron said, "we should consider every theory, no matter how far-fetched. And since it's getting late, maybe we should hold off on killing each other and plan what we're going to do next."

He was so logical. It made me want to jump him.

"I need to talk to Bryan," I said, shaking off that thought. "Maybe he saw something. But there's no way it'll happen tonight. I guess it'll have to wait until after we get back to school. Damn it."

"I'll keep digging into Holly's background. After I do my algebra homework." Jonah whooped and pumped his fist a few times before he scampered back in through the window. Apparently, he was one of those lunatics who got drunk on adrenaline. And he needed a real girlfriend. Desperately.

"What do you want me to do, Kate?" Aaron asked.

I wanted him to profess his undying love. But I asked him to drive me to the hospital after school the next day instead.

"Sure," he said.

He slipped his arms around me from behind, pulling my head back to rest against his chest. I could hear his heartbeat and smell the clean cotton of his shirt. Hundreds of questions bombarded my brain; it was embarrassing that so many of them centered on our relationship when I should have been more worried about the serial killer. One of the major drawbacks of being a teenage girl. Really, if I could have transplanted my brain into a fancy robot, life would have been much easier.

And I would have been able to fly, which would be really cool.

"Hey. What are you thinking about?" Aaron murmured.

"Um . . ." I pulled away reluctantly. "Just trying to figure out how to convince the authorities that these cases are connected. If I could get Dr. Burr out of jail, that would be nice."

He frowned. "You don't ever rest, do you?"

"Not really."

He took me by the shoulders. The kiss was so soft and gentle that it shouldn't have made my blood pressure shoot up into hypertension territory, but it did anyway. I pushed him back onto the shingles, scraping my forearms but not really caring. My mouth pressed against his, and now the kiss wasn't so gentle anymore. His hands were on my hips; I practically plastered myself to his torso. We hadn't gone any further than kissing, but suddenly I wanted to. Very badly.

"You should go inside," he said softly.

"That would be responsible," I agreed.

"Yeah."

"And warmer."

He laughed, pulling me close. The steam from our breath curled together, and we managed to find a way to stay warm for a little while longer.

CHAPTER
eleven

When I woke up the next morning, the light was all wrong. Not that I have anything against light in general, except that it wasn't supposed to be blazing out my eyeballs at this point in the day.

"Aw, crap!" I yelled, sitting bolt upright and checking the clock. It was indeed very late. I'd have to skip washing my hair, but maybe if I got dressed fast enough, I'd be able to grab a cup of coffee.

I threw something on and thundered down the stairs while trying to line up the buttons on my shirt correctly, but that was a lot more difficult than it sounds. So I really wasn't looking where I was going when I ran smack into my father in the hallway and nearly knocked him on his back.

"Sorry, Dad!" I grabbed his shoulders like that would keep

him upright. "I woke up late because of the whole thing with Bryan, and I'm just so tired, and I can't get this stupid shirt buttoned right, and . . ."

And then, I'm not proud of it, but I cried. It had nothing to do with the shirt. It was just that I couldn't stand one more thing going wrong.

Dad handed me a tissue, and I blew my nose with humiliating volume.

"Tell me what happened with Bryan." He sat on the stairs and patted the spot next to him. I curled up next to him, and he put an arm around me.

I told him everything, except for the bits where Aaron and I made out on our shingles, because even I have limits. It felt good to get things off my chest, even though I knew it meant I'd be late to catch the bus, and Mrs. Gilbert would be upset, and maybe she'd find out about Dr. Burr being in police custody. It was only a matter of time before the cops released his name. But those things didn't seem so important right now. Why was I rushing off to a mentorship program when I had no bleeping mentor?

"So how is Bryan doing?" Dad asked when I was done talking.

He was taking things awfully well. Then again, he was used to my status as the go-to person for various medical complaints. I'd spent half of Thanksgiving dinner on the phone with my aunt. She'd been convinced Uncle Jimmy was having a heart attack, but it turned out that he'd just had food poisoning from a bad can of Spam.

Personally, I couldn't believe I was related to a Spam eater, but that was beside the point.

"I don't know." I wiped my nose with my sleeve, and he handed me another tissue. "I'll try to text Rocky on the way to the FDA program. Can you drive me?"

"Or . . . ," he said thoughtfully, "I could drop you off at the hospital and you can go visit him yourself. I'll call the school office and let them know you'll go to your program after that, and you can catch the school bus back to classes when you're done. I know this program means a lot to you, pumpkin, but you're not going to be able to concentrate until you know your friend is okay. I know I wouldn't."

I considered it for about a half a second. "Yeah. That's exactly what I'll do. Thanks, Dad."

He ruffled my hair. I endured it, just this once. He'd earned it.

After some texting back and forth, Rocky had agreed to meet me in the hospital lobby. It took some careful maneuvering to make it through the revolving doors with a travel mug of coffee, a plastic bag containing a change of clothes for her, and my overstuffed backpack, but I managed. Rocky was slumped on one of the uncomfortable-looking sofas by the front doors.

"Thanks for coming," she said, bounding to her feet.

"Are you okay? Is Bryan okay?" I demanded, shoving the bag at her. "And here's some clean clothes. I know you didn't go home last night."

"You are officially the best friend in the history of the universe." She hugged me. "Let's go upstairs so I can change. And he's better than expected. A lot better. That's what I wanted to show you."

"What do you mean, he's better?" A jolt of fear ran through me. I really hoped I hadn't conducted a completely unnecessary surgery on one of my friends. If I had, I'd never forgive myself. But then I thought about how Bryan's neck had felt like someone dropped a bowling ball on it from a second-story window, and I realized there was no way I'd overreacted. I really had to stop flipping out so much.

"I can't tell you," Rocky said. "You've just got to see for yourself."

No amount of prodding would get her to talk, so I waited. It didn't take long for us to get to Bryan's room; our hospital wasn't all that big. It only had three floors, and one of them was dedicated to labor and delivery. I knew these things. I stalked the candy stripers in my spare time. They'd probably come to entirely the wrong conclusion about me, but that was okay.

When we went into Bryan's room, Rocky made a beeline for the bathroom.

"Take a look," she said. "I just really want to change into something clean. Mrs. R kept telling me to go home, but she's meeting with his doctors right now, and I didn't want him to wake up without anybody here."

I slowly approached the bed. Bryan was stretched out under the covers, resting peacefully. The monitors showed stable respiration and pulse; the IV dripped saline in a slow but steady rhythm. The pen had been replaced by a tracheotomy tube; they'd probably keep that in place until they could reconstruct the windpipe and its supporting cartilage. I felt absurdly relieved to see it; it meant my crichoidectomy hadn't been completely unnecessary.

"What did you want to show me?" I called toward the bathroom.

"Check out his neck."

Rocky came back out in one of my Bayview sweatshirts and a pair of too-long sweats. She perched on the end of a puke-colored chair at the side of the bed.

I looked. There wasn't much to see, just a smooth expanse of skin broken by the white bandages holding the tube in place. I was about to ask exactly what I should be looking for when it hit me.

In the gravel lot, I had realized Bryan's windpipe was smashed because of the marks on his neck. Those things usually take days to fade, and I didn't see any.

"Where'd the purpura go?" I demanded, bending over him. Getting closer didn't miraculously make them appear. Big surprise.

"Purpura?"

"The red marks on his neck."

"They went away," replied Rocky. "The doctors are really freaked out about it. They won't transfer him to University until they can explain what happened. I think they're worried about a lawsuit or something."

"So they can't explain it?" I looked a little closer. The skin was smooth and completely unblemished. Not even a bruise, and that didn't make any sense at all.

"They tried to scan him again, but the scanner won't work on him. The films keep coming out all white. Bryan's mom is meeting with them now, but I thought maybe you'd be able to explain it."

I was about to protest that there was no way I'd know what was going on if the doctors didn't, but then I heard something that caught my attention. The faintest sound came from the bed, or somewhere near it. I held up my hand for quiet. We stood there motionless for a minute or two, my ears straining to catch it again.

There it was. Under the hollow sound of air moving through the tube, I heard it. A quiet crackle, like Rice Krispies in milk.

"What is it?" Rocky crept toward the bed.

I shook my head. I didn't know what it was. I'd never heard anything like this coming from a human body before.

I knew I shouldn't touch him. It wasn't safe, although if he had any communicable diseases I'd probably managed to infect myself when I'd given him a crichoidectomy without gloves. I could accidentally do more damage just by touching him, but I had to know. The tips of my fingers quivered in the air, and I forced them to stillness. I placed them, feather-light, on the side of his neck.

His skin quivered like a colony of tiny ants scurried underneath it.

My hand jerked back, and I rubbed my fingers together in an attempt to get rid of the creepy-crawly feeling. Then the back of my neck started to itch; it was obviously psychosomatic, but I scratched anyway.

"What?" Rocky demanded.

"What what?"

"What were you listening to?"

She spoke with exaggerated patience, so exaggerated that I knew she wasn't feeling patient at all. Unfortunately, I couldn't answer the question. I had no idea what the noise was. If I didn't know better, I'd think his neck was repairing itself.

Luckily, I knew that was impossible. Just like zombies.

I shook my head. "I'm not sure what it is yet. You can check it out for yourself if you want. I need to try and sneak a peek at Bryan's chart. Somehow."

I had to admit the idea didn't fill me with glee. I was not double-oh-seven material. I was more like double-oh-klutzy. Or double-oh-going-to-get-thrown-out-of-the-hospital.

"Mrs. R is meeting with the medical team down the hall. They probably have it down there. You think they'd let you look at it if you asked?" Rocky asked.

"Probably not. But it won't hurt to try."

I let myself out into the hall. It was deserted, which seemed strange for this time of day. There must have been cake in the break room, or maybe a freak zombie attack on the second floor.

I tiptoed up to the nurses' station and felt like a complete idiot when I saw that it was empty. I'd just tiptoed needlessly. I glanced over my shoulder to make sure Rocky hadn't witnessed this latest bonehead move on my part, but Bryan's door was closed. Whew.

When I turned back to the desk, there was a nurse standing in front of me.

"What are you doing?" She folded her arms and stared me down with squinty, piggish eyes.

"I . . . you . . ." I couldn't seem to form a coherent sentence at first but finally managed to blurt out, "Did you just beam down from the mother ship?"

"Pardon me?" she asked, but it sounded like a demand more than a question.

"There wasn't anyone here just a second ago, and then I turned around, and you . . ." I had to stop babbling before she smacked me. From the look on her face, I figured I had about one point two seconds. "Sorry. You surprised me."

"This is a restricted floor, and visiting hours aren't until ten a.m."

"I know!" I said quickly. "I know. But I just dropped off some clothes for Bryan's girlfriend, and I wanted to let Mrs. Rodriguez know that . . . uh . . . I'm taking her downstairs for breakfast. She's meeting with the doctors, right? I didn't want to interrupt."

"Yes, she is. They won't be done for a while yet." I watched her eyes carefully; they darted to a closed door down the hallway and back. I'd have bet my booty that was where the doctors were meeting with Mrs. Rodriguez.

"Well, could you give her the message when she's done?" I chirped.

"I'll give her the message," she muttered. Then she stared at me like my continued existence was a personal affront.

I smiled at her with as much innocence as I could scrape up and went back down the hallway. Once I was out of sight of the nurses' station, I plastered myself against the wall, barely restraining the urge to start humming pseudo–spy music under my breath. I had to listen in on that meeting. Some people might have said it was none of my business, but those kinds of people didn't cure zombie infestations. Or non-werewolf ones.

Unfortunately, in order to get to what I assumed was the meeting room, I'd have to double back past the nurses' station. But it was worth the risk. Bryan's mom would happily tell me all about the meeting if I asked her to, but she might miss some essential piece of info that would explain it all. Besides, the whole waiting thing would require actual *waiting*, and I didn't deal well with that.

So I dropped to my hands and knees and crawled down the hallway, hoping that nurse didn't come out to empty the bedpans. If she did, I figured I'd tell her I lost my lucky pen.

Naturally, now that I'd come up with a decent alibi, she didn't catch me. I crawled all the way down the hallway, past the nurses' station, and down to the door without being discovered. Of course, now it felt like my knees had been repeatedly bashed by an ill-tempered dwarf with a hammer, but that was okay. I was a semi-secret agent; I could handle those kinds of things.

I put my ear to the door. Unfortunately, it was one of those heavy-duty hospital doors; they make them pretty solid so you can't listen through them. So I stood up, prayed that no one happened to be looking in my direction, and peeked through the gap in the window blinds.

There was no one there. Mucho anticlimactic.

I tried the handle; the door opened soundlessly. I crept into a small room dominated by a circular table and a couple of abstract pastel paintings that looked like teeth wearing parachutes. Too freaky. Half-empty coffee cups littered the tabletop. They were still lukewarm. Mrs. Rodriguez and co. must have just left a few minutes earlier.

The computer stood against the far wall. I knew it was futile. Hospital systems don't dork around; they've got security out the ying yang. The screen had one of those blurring frames on it that makes it impossible to read unless you're sitting directly in front of it. Good thing I was back in epileptic remission, because the random fuzzy flashes probably would have sent me straight to neurological crazytown otherwise.

I nudged the mouse without much hope. And for the first time ever, I was quite happy that our hospital was technologically backward. Because the screen flashed to life, and Bryan's record still stood open.

It looked like they'd just done a series of CT scans about an hour earlier. CTs give you a nice high-def look at bones and soft tissue and seemed like just the thing I was looking for. But all the images were bad. Totally white, despite their low exposure. So unless Bryan had turned into a huge blob of bone when I wasn't looking, there was something seriously wrong.

The only thing I could think of that could cause something like this would be metal. Metal objects like jewelry really screw with the images. But to turn the whole film white, he'd have to wear enough necklaces to make the average rap star quiver with envy.

Of course, the metal thing made me think of the magnetic blood. If the blood sample contained metal, and Bryan's CT was messed up because of some kind of metal contaminant, I had to conclude he was infected with whatever his attacker had. Forget werewolves; with my luck he'd turn into a cyborg and start shooting lasers out his eyeballs.

I scanned through the records, looking for blood cultures, but someone grabbed me by the arm before I got that far. Just my luck; it was my favorite nurse.

"I thought I made it clear that visiting hours haven't started yet." She pulled me out of the chair and "assisted" me down the hallway.

"I dropped my lucky pen?" I said, but we both knew I was full of it.

This was how I managed to get myself escorted to the front door of the hospital. I won't say I got thrown out, because there was no actual throwing involved. There was some dragging, though. A lot of dragging.

CHAPTER
twelve

Since I wasn't exactly welcome in the hospital anymore, I texted Rocky and swung through the morgue on my way to the bus stop. It was empty except for the secretaries, and they hadn't seen Sebastian yet this morning. I couldn't blame the guy for sleeping in because, well, that would have been awfully hypocritical.

I was pretty excited to see Aaron, especially after the night before. Should I say something to acknowledge what had happened? It's not like we'd gone all the way on my roof, because I'm not that tacky, and I don't really think shingles and bare skin go well together. But it still felt like something monumental had happened. Something that needed to be recognized.

So I entered the hospital lobby with a whole crazy mess of emotions—nervousness, excitement, happiness, fear. I wanted to sit next to Aaron on the bus with his leg touching mine and feel that thrill again.

Then I saw him, sitting on one of the benches near the doors, bundled up in his black winter coat with the scarf I'd gotten him for Christmas wound casually around his neck. His head was thrown back, and he was laughing at something. Elle sat next to him, her face turned up to his. It was impossible to miss her expression of vapid adoration. As I watched, she launched herself onto his lap and shoved her tongue in his mouth.

My vision went red.

I stalked toward them. Aaron pushed her away, but she obviously wasn't getting the picture. She twined her fingers in his hair. I hated her. And while I could understand him not wanting to screw up his opportunity with his orthopedist, I'd had it.

"Get your slutty hands off my boyfriend before I rip them off you!" I yelled.

Every head in the lobby twisted in my direction. The bus pulled up outside with a loud belch of exhaust, but no one moved a muscle. Well, one guy did. He got out his phone and started taking video. I think he expected a catfight, and I was honestly tempted to give him one.

Elle leapt off Aaron's lap and made a little screamy face. I didn't even want to waste my time with her.

"Aaron, you have one minute to explain, and that's it," I said.

He stood up, clearing his throat nervously.

"I told her not to," he said. "I didn't kiss her back. I'm sorry,

Kate. She took me by surprise; you had to see that. . . ." He shook his head. "I don't know what to do. She won't take the hint."

"You've got a choice here." My voice wavered, but I was otherwise strangely calm. I didn't care if I was still marginally geeky. Or if my social skills still needed polishing, or if sometimes I felt like I was speaking a totally different language than the rest of the world. I was still a million times cooler than her, and he should have known that. "It's her or me. If you want to see her outside this program, that's your choice. But if it happens again, you need to know that I'll dump your butt so fast you'll crack your tailbone."

He gaped at me. So did Elle.

"You'll dump me?" Aaron asked, like it was a foreign concept that he'd never had cause to consider before. Probably he hadn't. Neither had I, but there's a first time for everything.

"You seem to think," I went on, "that I have no balls. But I'm willing to stand up for us. The question is whether you're willing to do the same."

I stared him down. The overhead lights glinted off his obnoxiously long eyelashes, and the downy hairs on his cheek glistened like he was a vampire who'd been rolling in a tween's secret glitter stash. I saw the jumpy tic of a muscle in his jaw, the telltale sign that he was nervous. But he didn't say anything. I wasn't sure if he was stunned or afraid that I might snap if he told me he was dumping me for Brain-Dead Barbie.

"Aaron!" she barked, waving her cell at him like it was a

mind-control device. "Get on the bus before she goes all psycho on you; I'll call the cops." She made a move for the door, but he didn't budge. "Aaron?"

I'd said what I needed to. I saw no sense in standing around until someone came to take me away to a place where the Happy Pills were plentiful and craft time was mandatory. Because really, I'd rather transplant my own spleen than subject myself to craft time.

I stalked away, or at least I started to. I only made it about five steps before I heard Aaron's voice, shaky and soft and nearly unrecognizable.

He said, "I really do love you, Kate."

It was almost enough to make me turn back around, throw myself at his feet, and cry. Almost. But I had a murderer to catch. Besides, anything he had to say was completely irrelevant. The only thing that was going to make this right was if he got rid of Elle for good. And if he couldn't or wouldn't, I knew what I had to do. I hated it, but I'd do it.

I went through the rest of the day like a zombie, minus the puking and cannibalistic tendencies. Kiki's locker was only two down from mine, and sometimes we ran into each other between classes. When she tapped me on the shoulder, it was two minutes until the seventh-period bell rang, and I was staring dully at my Latin book and wondering if it was even worth bringing it to class because no way was I going to register a single word Mrs. Cooperider said.

"Hey, Kate!" Kiki said, turning her lock. "Did you pick up the chairs for the Rockathon tomorrow night?"

I stared at her blankly.

"Please tell me you're kidding." Evidently, the look on my face wasn't too reassuring on that account, because she threw up her hands. "Look, I don't mind helping you with your event, but this is turning into me running the entire thing! And I've got my own stuff to do, you know."

"I'm sorry." I shook my head. "I've got a lot on my mind. I'll get them tonight."

Maybe Rocky would drive me. Or Jonah. Because I certainly wasn't going to call Aaron. I was waiting for him to make the first move. But why hadn't he done it already? I kept rushing back to my locker between classes, thinking I'd find a note from him or see him waiting there for me, but it didn't happen. Was he really going to choose Elle over me? And how could I be obsessing over this when a not-a-werewolf was killing people? My priorities were crap, and knowing that only made me feel worse.

For once, Kiki didn't seem to notice how upset I was, which was probably a good thing, because I had this aversion to public tears and I was going to cry if anybody asked me what was wrong. All she did was thrust a sheet of paper at me. I shoved it into my backpack without even looking at it.

"It's Trey Black's address. His parents are lending us the chairs," she said. "Just in case you lost it."

"Thanks," I said, but it was too late. She'd already flounced off.

* * *

By the time detention was over, I was ready to go home and bury myself in homework. I felt pulled in so many directions by what other people wanted. What about what I wanted? Was I going to spend my whole life trying to save the world and sacrificing all the things that were important to me in the process? Because I had no doubt that Aaron wouldn't be avoiding me if I'd been a more attentive girlfriend. If I hadn't been so sucked up in tracking down murderers and zombies and all kinds of stuff that wasn't even my job. Maybe I should just leave these things to the "experts."

My dad picked me up after school, which was a bonus because Kiki wasn't speaking to me. And he was right on time too. When I walked out to the school parking lot, his Nissan hybrid was parked right in the middle of the fire lane.

Jonah rolled down the passenger-side window to wave at me. "You're in the back," he yelled.

I threw my backpack in and myself in after it.

"So," Dad said, pulling away from the curb, "what are we eating tonight, Kate? Indian? Mexican? Or did you go for one of our old standbys?"

"I have no idea what you're talking about, Dad."

He arched his brows at me in the rearview mirror. "You were in charge of making the reservations for Mom's welcome home dinner. Please don't tell me you forgot."

"Fine," I growled. "I won't tell you."

It didn't take long to find the number for Shalimar, Mom's

favorite Indian restaurant, on my phone. And it was easy to get a reservation, since it was only Thursday.

"Done." I snapped my phone closed and stared out the window for the rest of the drive while Dad and Jonah discussed *Mythbusters* episodes in excruciating detail.

The sulking got pretty tough to maintain once we parked in the short-term lot and made our way into the crowded airport terminal. It was impossible not to get excited; I hadn't seen my mom in six months except for on the computer screen. She'd wanted to come back after the zombie fiasco, but by that time it was all over, and it just didn't seem to make sense to screw up her sabbatical just so she could come hold my hand.

Now I couldn't wait to see her.

That explains why I found myself running as soon as she cleared security, like I was an actress in one of those movies where everyone's dashing into each other's arms in slo-mo while violins play in the background. She threw her arms around me. I had to lean a little to put my head on her shoulder. That was new.

I didn't let go until Dad cleared his throat.

"I missed you," I said, pulling back. I would have let go entirely, but she snagged the sleeve of my coat first. Her eyes were keen beneath thick, slightly smudged glasses.

"Are you okay?" she asked.

This was my chance to vent, and I knew I should take it. It made a lot more sense than huffing around like a drama queen. But this really wasn't the time or the place for it. Jonah and Dad were waiting impatiently; they'd missed her too. And besides, I could take care of myself.

"I'm fine," I said. "Welcome home."

But I made a mental note to unload as soon as I got the chance. Mom tended to give pretty good advice when you could get her head out of a beaker. Unfortunately, I could barely get a word in edgewise over the next hour, because Jonah had to give her a play-by-play rundown of everything he'd done in the past six months, like we hadn't been Skyping with her twice a week the entire time she'd been gone. By the time he was done monopolizing her, I was already halfway through my tandoori chicken.

"I wonder what's in the dessert case today," Dad said, pushing his chair back from the table.

Jonah stood up. "Wait for me. Man, I hope they have that fig and honey ice cream."

"I think I'll follow." Dad patted Mom's hand. "Give you two girls a chance to catch up too."

Mom's eyes followed them as they crossed the restaurant and started loudly debating the contents of the stuffed dessert case. I noticed wrinkles on her face that I'd never seen before, and her wild curly hair was longer than it had been when she'd left. Somehow, the differences seemed bigger now that I was seeing her in person.

"You've been quiet tonight." She took a sip of her lassi and looked me over.

"I guess I've got a lot on my mind."

"I'd been hoping that Aaron would be joining us. I've heard so much about him that I feel like I know him already."

The lump in my throat was very tough to swallow. "I don't know if that's going to happen, Mom. Things aren't going too well with us right now."

In the background, I could hear my dad interrogating the waitstaff on the differences between Indian and American ice cream in an embarrassingly loud voice.

"Do you ever have a hard time balancing it all?" I blurted out. "Because I suck at it. It feels like the minute I fix one thing, something else has gone to crap. I feel like I must not be trying hard enough."

"Somehow I doubt that," she smiled. "But yes, I find it tough to say no to things. Which explains why I took the visiting professorship in Germany. I loved the work, but being away from all of you was miserable."

"So I just have to deal with it?"

"No, you have to figure out what you're willing to sacrifice. I'll never keep the cleanest house. I have a small number of friends, but they're the ones who really mean a lot to me. I'm terrible at trivia. I don't watch TV or craft or take up hobbies unless I'm really interested in them. The bulk of my time is reserved for the two things I love the most—my family and my job."

"It's that easy, huh?"

"Well," she said, the corners of her mouth quirking up, "it's not exactly rocket science."

"Did someone say 'rocket science'?" Dad walked back to our table and planted a kiss on Mom's cheek. "Coincidentally, I happen to be a rocket scientist! Did you know that?"

"Yes, dear." Mom grinned at me.

I forced a smile. Maybe she was right—all I had to do was prioritize. And repair my relationship, organize a fund-raiser, solve a medical mystery, and catch a murderer.

Easy.

CHAPTER
thirteen

Mom drove me to the morgue on Friday, so I didn't have to ride the bus. I really needed to talk to Aaron, but I supposed a couple of hours wasn't really going to make that much of a difference.

I'd woken up with a clear plan, so I felt pretty good as I pushed open the door to the morgue. I'd check to see if either of our two corpses had the skin ants like Bryan. I'd find out if there had been hairs at either of the other crime scenes. And then I'd amaze Aaron with my powers of deduction, and he'd realize I was the only girl for him. There were holes in this plan, but I was willing to improvise.

Dr. Burr was not part of said plan, so when I pushed open the door and saw him washing his hands at the prep sink, I nearly fell over.

"Dr. Burr?" I gasped. "What are you doing here?"

"Working." He shut off the faucets with his elbows and meticulously dried his hands with a paper towel. "There was another attack behind a restaurant on Wednesday. Apparently, some enterprising soul did a crichoidectomy with a pen cap right in the middle of the parking lot and saved the fellow's life. The detectives found hair that matched a few strands found at the other scene. They released me last night and cleared me to autopsy the bodies. I'm quite motivated to catch this killer, given all the inconvenience he's caused us."

It was so good to see him that I was getting a little teary. It seemed silly to get all overemotional over a guy had who mentored me for about fifteen minutes so far, but I couldn't help myself.

"I'm rather surprised to see you." But he didn't look upset; he smiled at me instead. "I figured you would have run for surgery by now."

"I wanted to see an autopsy."

"Well, now's your chance. Sebastian called in sick today. The stress has gotten to him, poor boy. Between this job and his internship over at Nanotech Industries, I think he works too hard."

"I didn't realize he worked somewhere else," I said, but I wasn't really paying attention, because I was in the process of putting on my very own sterile gown. And nitrile gloves. And a face mask. I looked like a real doctor, and it was every bit as awesome as I'd thought it would be.

For a while, I got lost in a haze of tissue condition and safety precautions and proper incision techniques. I wasn't allowed to do any cutting by myself, especially on the murder victims, but Dr. Burr put his hand over mine and guided the scalpel for me. And really, he didn't have to do much guiding. It was like my hand knew exactly where to go and how much pressure to bear.

We autopsied Herbie first, although Dr. Burr was still calling him John Doe. I wasn't so sure how he'd react to the news that I was investigating on my own, so I made sure not to let anything slip. And then we did Holly. By the time it was all over, we were staring at each other in complete and utter confusion.

"This doesn't make any sense," Dr. Burr said for the umpteenth time, throwing up his hands.

"Tell me about it." I paced back and forth, chewing on the end of my braid. "Okay, let's talk it out. Maybe we'll come up with something." He gestured for me to go on. "Here's what we know. Both of the deceased were victims of brutal attacks. The police reports note extensive blood loss and open wounds. Their injuries were presumably enough to kill them. But on autopsy, both victims are found to be in perfect health, with no signs of bruising and not a single break of the skin. Not even a shaving nick."

"Holly supposedly had her appendix out, according to her medical records, but there's no scar and the appendix is present. I'll double check with the mother once she arrives later today," added Dr. Burr. "I've seen a few cases in which they've grown back, but it's rare."

"Right. So either the police were hallucinating, or somehow the injuries healed themselves. . . ."

Dr. Burr jerked to attention, looking at my face. "You've just thought of something."

"Maybe."

I moved forward, hesitantly putting my fingers to Holly's neck, her arms, her hips. The skin was cold but pliant. I didn't feel anything moving around inside her, but maybe that wasn't such a bad thing. If she had whatever Bryan had, the ants had already done their job. They'd fixed everything.

"Well?" Dr. Burr prompted.

"Let me try one more thing." I pulled off my gloves and dumped them into the infectious waste bin. "Do you have a magnet handy?"

Now he was really looking curious, but he went into the storage room and pulled a magnet off the fridge. It said, Pathologists—WE SEE DEAD PEOPLE.

I snorted. "Funny. Now let's see if this works or not."

When I set the magnet down on the specimen tray next to the vials of blood we'd taken from Holly, nothing happened. This had to work; I moved the magnet a little closer. And then the vial of blood rolled across the tray and stuck to the magnet with a clack.

"Magnetic blood?" asked Dr. Burr, his voice hushed with awe.

"Exactly."

The door buzzer picked that moment to go off, and we stared at it with identical expressions of exasperation. Dr. Burr got up to answer it, mumbling words under his breath that I was sure my delicate underage ears didn't need to hear.

"I hope this is good," he said into the intercom.

"Dr. Burr?" came the crackle-voiced reply. "This is Detective Lynn Despain. I was hoping to talk to you."

It felt like the universe was telling me to spill everything. So after she came in, I did.

Well, not *everything* everything. I skipped the relationship bits and the neurotic bits and the part where I got thrown out of the hospital, but I told them everything else about the magnetic blood and the mutant hair and the accelerated healing. All of it.

"And, you know," I said, "I'm pretty logical, and I don't believe in ghosts and stuff. But this really does sound like the werewolf legends, doesn't it? You've got the hair and the super strength and the super speed and the healing. The only thing that doesn't fit is the blood."

Dr. Burr patted my hand. "I'm sure we can come up with another explanation, Kate. I'll send the blood to toxicology. Perhaps this is a very extreme case of lead poisoning."

But Despain didn't seem so sure. "I wouldn't write her off just yet, Doc," she said. "I'm sure there's a logical cause underlying it, just as there was with the zombie phenomenon, but that doesn't mean she's wrong."

"Thanks for the vote of confidence," I said.

"I'm going to tell our lab techs about this and see what they can come up with," she said. "We'll look into this, Kate. In the meantime, let me get you back to school."

I should have been relieved, right? School was where I belonged, especially if I intended to set some priorities. I needed to see Aaron and Rocky and Kiki and to be a normal teenager for a while.

But I wasn't relieved at all.

When Despain dropped me off in her squad car, I made my way toward the front doors of the school. But as soon as she was out of sight, I veered off into the parking lot. Luckily, it was the middle of fifth period, and too cold for anyone to eat out in the quad. Otherwise, there would have been no way for me to sneak off unseen.

Jonah had given me a copy of his keys after I'd left my backpack in his car over the weekend one time and woke him up before noon. He was going to regret that when he found out that I took his car. But desperate times require desperate measures. Like driving without a license and semi-stealing your brother's car.

I still couldn't believe his luck. I had a cruddy old car, not like I was complaining as long as it got me from point A to B without breaking down. But he'd lucked into a cute, if aged, two-door convertible. And it was all because I'd cured the son of the guy who ran the local used-car dealership during the zombie apocalypse. Sure, Jonah drove me around since I was still license-impaired, but that didn't change the fact that the car should have been mine.

So I drove off, über-tempted to put the hood down. But it was starting to snow—little flakes that couldn't decide if they wanted to fall down or fly sideways. I decided against it.

At the intersection of Wills and State, I hesitated. Left toward my house or right toward the hospital? I flicked on the left-hand blinker. Maybe Bryan was conscious. Maybe he'd seen his attacker.

Maybe he could identify them, werewolf or no.

CHAPTER
fourteen

Skipping school was a little nerve-wracking, but I'd done it during the zombie outbreak, and it seemed to me that the key was to act like you were exactly where you were supposed to be. So I walked into the hospital without looking back. As I emerged from the elevator onto Bryan's floor, I heard a loud buzzing from the nurses' station. "Looks like that darned sensor on bed twelve slipped off again," someone was saying. "Do we have another one somewhere?"

I walked up to the desk just in time to see two nurses disappear into the back. Perfect. I went to Bryan's room. The light above the door beeped and flashed incessantly. Because I was a genius, I concluded that he must be in bed twelve with the malfunctioning sensor. Of course, the number twelve on the door didn't hurt.

I silently thanked the gods that my epilepsy was under control; otherwise, those flashy lights would have probably sent me into total neurological meltdown. And then the nurses would have sent me down to Emergency, where some sleep-deprived intern would tell me what I already knew, which was that I had just had a seizure. Then I would make some smart-ass comment about how I already knew that because I had more than five brain cells, and then he'd burst into tears and leave the room. I knew these things. I had experience.

So it was a really good thing I hadn't had a seizure in months.

I reached the door, turned the handle, and pushed it open, since that's pretty much standard operating procedure as far as doors are concerned. A monstrosity leapt out at me. It looked like Bryan, if you added about seventeen pounds of dark brown hair and a Klingon forehead. His face was all bulgy and distorted. I couldn't decide if his teeth were elongated or if they just looked that way because he was baring them at me.

He was a werewolf. Jonah was never going to let me hear the end of this, assuming that I lived. And if I died, he'd probably taunt me via Ouija board.

Before I realized what was happening, Bryan barreled into me, forcing all the air from my chest in a high-pitched squeak. My very brief martial arts training flashed through my mind; I knew I ought to roll, or strike, or grapple, or something other than be thrown around like a rag doll. I settled for stumbling backward, trying to suck air into my lungs.

He grabbed me by the arms and slammed me against the

wall. My vision swam, and when it cleared, his face was inches from mine. His nostrils flared as he took in my scent, but his eyes showed no sign of recognition or even coherent thought. His brow was drawn down into a simian squint, giving him an almost Cro-Magnon look underneath the fur.

"Bryan," I said softly. "It's me. Kate. I'm your friend. I'm here to help you."

He growled, deep and low in his throat. I heard footsteps coming down the hall, shouts of alarm that sounded like they were coming from miles away. He threw me toward the nurses' station, and I sailed through the air in what felt like slow motion. I had way too much time to contemplate how badly it was going to hurt when I landed. And then the world exploded with pain.

I came to with my cheek pillowed on cold tile. You'd think that would have been uncomfortable, but my head wouldn't stop throbbing, so the chill felt pretty good. There was something in my eye; I wiped it off with a shaky hand. It tinted my fingers blue. And my arm was all blue too. Peachy.

"Oh my god!" someone exclaimed, and I heard rapid footsteps coming in my direction. I wanted to warn whoever it is that there was a werewolf on the loose, but I couldn't make my mouth work yet.

A blob came into my field of vision, but without my glasses, I had no idea who it was. I was pretty sure it wasn't Bryan—unless he was trying to fake me out by putting on a pair of hot pink scrubs. I tried to focus, but I'd whacked my head pretty hard during the struggle. And when I say "struggle," I mean "part where I got my butt kicked."

It was the same nurse who had thrown me out before. She checked my pulse with a gentle hand. I did nothing. Frankly, I was content to lie there on the floor for the next eternity, or at least until my head stopped hurting.

"Can you hear me?" she asked. I nodded and immediately regretted it.

Another nurse came running down the hall, and there was a rapid exchange of details between them before she went off to call for a gurney to take me down to the ER. A third nurse ran into Bryan's room and then down the hallway. She was probably calling security to notify them of a missing patient. I didn't think they'd catch him, but it was a nice thought.

Then we went through the drill where my nurse asked me for the name of the president, and how many fingers she was holding up, all the usual questions to see if I was oriented to person, place, and time. I was tempted to screw with her, but then I'd probably end up strapped to an MRI machine or something. That would have interfered with my plans to determine how Bryan had contracted a case of raging werewolfism. So I concentrated on answering with as little sarcasm as possible. It was a lot tougher than I expected.

"So what was that thing?" she finally asked.

I'd been expecting the question but couldn't think of an

answer that didn't sound like complete lunacy. I couldn't explain my werewolf theory yet except to say I thought he was one and was sure there was a scientifically feasible explanation for it. That wasn't the most satisfactory answer in the world, though. Probably the basic facts were least likely to get me into trouble.

"I don't really know," I mumbled. "I opened the door, and someone jumped out. It all happened so fast that I didn't even get a good look at him . . . her . . . it."

"Well, they threw you all the way down the hallway." She ran gentle fingers down the side of my skull. It hurt, but not enough to make me scream. Close.

"I landed pretty hard, huh?"

She snorted. "You put a huge hole in the wall, so I'd say that's an understatement."

I twisted my head, ignoring the combined protests of my cranium and the nurse, and barely made out what looked like a hole in the drywall. At least I no longer needed to worry that I was turning into an X-Man. I hadn't inexplicably turned blue; I was just covered in powdered wall.

She put her hands on either side of my head and frowned. "Stop moving. You could have a neck injury."

"I don't have a neck injury."

"Humor me."

We sat there for another minute or two, and soon I heard a repetitive squeaking that could only herald the approach of a gurney. I looked up at her. "Thank you." Because sure, she'd thrown me out of the hospital yesterday, but she was like a totally differ-ent person today. Maybe this was the good twin and yesterday I'd met the bad one. Or maybe she just didn't recognize me under all the blue.

"You're welcome," she said. "I figure I owed you, anyway."

I guess I was more memorable than I thought.

They took me straight into a bay in the emergency depart-ment. Getting thrown into a wall gave me a certain amount of notoriety; a lot of people stopped by to look me over, but when I tried to talk to them, the only thing they'd say was that the doctor would see me soon. It didn't take long for me to get impatient, because my head wouldn't stop throbbing. The least they could do was give me a little pain medicine—not a lot, because I needed to be able to think straight if I was going to capture the werewolf.

I had nothing better to do, and I needed to distract myself from the pain radiating from the back of my skull, so I started thinking through the facts. Something had infected Bryan, and I definitely didn't buy into the whole bitten-by-a-wolf theory. No, whatever this was had also made his blood magnetic. That meant it wasn't a virus; it had to be something metal, and something small. . . .

Then it clicked. Sebastian was an intern at Nanotech Indus-tries. Nanomedicine was making leaps and bounds all the time; it was the only reasonable explanation I could come up with.

The whole theory of nanomedicine is that you can use micro-scopic machines to stimulate the body to be more efficient. You can't make someone fly, because the body can't do that already. But you might make them heal stronger, run faster, hit harder, and so on.

Bryan clearly was infected with nanobots, and I'd found all that blood all over him. If the infection spread via bodily fluids, that would explain how he'd contracted it. Same thing with Holly and her brother. That would explain how they'd healed after the fact—it took a while for the bots to start working. And apparently, they also provided a highly effective cure for baldness.

The theory made me feel tons better. No, I still didn't know who the murderer was, but I had a lead. I could get to the bottom of this. Maybe the whole situation was some strange industrial accident. It was just a case of accidental nanobotting.

I wasn't looking forward to telling Rocky that her boyfriend had contracted a bad case of werebots. Probably the best thing I could do was get it over with quick. I dug my cell out of the pocket of my hoodie and called her, but it went straight to voice mail. Either she was on the hospital floor or at school; neither of those places was cell compatible.

I sat up, ignoring the thunder in my head, and loosened the brace from around my neck. Now was not the time to be chilling in the ED. I had to hunt down Sebastian and find out exactly what these nanobots did and how to stop them. I wasn't going to wait for the doctors to put me through about six hundred X-rays to tell me what I already knew: I didn't have a neck injury. No numbness, no loss of sensation, and no loss of motor control. At worst, I had an isolated skull fracture.

I also had a werewolf to catch.

I swept the privacy curtain open and found myself staring at a nose. Said nose was attached to a guy in a white coat. I recognized him immediately; I had made him cry the last time I was here, after the zombie attack went down.

"Oh." The white-coated intern heaved a huge, melodramatic sigh. "It's you."

"I know." I started to walk around him. "Excuse me."

"Does this mean that you're refusing treatment?"

I nodded, and the guy actually clapped, he was so happy.

"That's the best news I've heard all day! Let me get you the paperwork to sign and you'll be on your way."

I would have berated him for his lack of professionalism, but I didn't have time. Besides, my head felt like it might fall off if I moved it too much, and then someone would mistake me for a zombie. I knew what happened to zombies. Firsthand, even.

"Get me some painkillers while you're at it," I called after him.

"Sure! I'm happy to help!" He skipped down the hallway. Apparently, I'd miraculously turned into one of those people who spread sunshine wherever they go. If I figured out who had made me like this, I'd hunt them down and punch them.

He returned quickly, holding a pair of paper cups, with a piece of paper tucked under one arm. The pills went straight into my mouth, but I didn't bother with the water. There are few skills that come with being an epileptic med-head, so I liked to employ them when I could.

Of course, once I dry-swallowed the pills, I realized I was

really thirsty. I drank the water anyway. And felt more than a little stupid.

The intern waved the treatment refusal in front of my face and practically begged me to sign. I wrote my name in my best unreadable physician scrawl and pushed past him.

I had too many things to do. I needed to hunt down Bryan and keep him from throwing people into walls. I needed to find Sebastian and learn about the nanobots. What I *really* needed was about a dozen clones—one to chase down Sebastian, one to find Bryan, one to take my bio test, and a bunch to obsess over Aaron. Unfortunately, all I had was an elf-obsessed little brother with a hero complex, a best friend who never answered her phone, and a boyfriend who might or might not have broken up with me. As far as posses went, it left room for improvement.

CHAPTER
fifteen

Since I had no idea where Bryan had gone and even less of an idea of what to do when I found him, I decided to hunt down Sebastian first. Dr. Burr probably had his home address, but if I went down to the morgue he'd also probably start asking uncomfortable questions like "Why aren't you in school?" and "You didn't steal your brother's car to get here, did you?" Maybe I could worm the address out of the people at Sebastian's other job. Heck, maybe he'd be there.

I passed Nanotech Industries all the time; it was housed in this funky glass building with a slanted roof right down the street from Legs and Eggs. I'd always wanted to go in there, but they didn't do tours. That was too bad, because I thought nanobots were freaking sweet. There was something sublimely awesome about robots so minuscule I couldn't see them without a microscope. I had read a huge article in the paper a couple of weeks before about these bots developed at Nanotech to increase things like muscle strength, response time, and recovery. They were only using them in animals, and human applications were probably years away, but I hoped the research would progress quickly enough that I got to use nanobots in my medical practice someday. In the meantime, the article hung on my wall with a big heart drawn around it.

Suddenly, I realized I was a huge, unobservant idiot. Nanotech Industries stood right across the empty lot where Bryan had been attacked. Sebastian had access to the nanobots through his internship. He knew Dr. Burr and probably had access to his swipe card. He'd recognized Holly.

Sebastian was the link between all the victims. I had a hard time picturing that concave-chested wimp as a murderous werewolf, but I had to admit that all the evidence was pointing in that direction.

Given that little revelation, it seemed very stupid to rush off to Nanotech without some kind of protection. If Sebastian was there and I said something to tick him off, he could wolf out at any second.

I'd been thinking through all of this as I hunched over the sink in the hospital bathroom, trying in vain to wash the drywall dust off. It just kept smearing around, leaving blue-tinged swirls on my skin. I'd sudsed up my arms for the fourth time when my phone started vibrating. It took some Cirque du Soleil–level contortion to get it out of my pocket without soaking my pants, but I managed.

"Yeah?" I set the phone on the countertop and continued to scrub. It looked like I might be doomed to a life of blue.

"Please tell me you have my car and are skipping class to hunt werewolves." It was Jonah. "Because if you don't, I think somebody stole it."

"Don't worry. I've got it."

"Oh good." He paused. "Although I'm going to kill you for scaring me like that. And then Mom and Dad are going to resurrect you and kill you again for driving without a license."

"Let me make it up to you," I said. "Can you think of an excuse and get out of class? Because I'd feel a lot better about werewolf hunting if I had backup."

"Really?" he squeaked. "I'll get out of Earth Sciences if I have to tunnel my way out with a spork. Meet you by the side doors in five?"

I looked critically at myself. Grains of blue powder stuck to the hairs on my arm; all I was doing was moving them around.

"Make it ten," I said. "Right now, I look like an X-Men reject, and I need a little time to remedy that."

"Today just keeps getting better and better," he said happily, and then he hung up.

One thing I'd discovered about convertibles—they're really drafty even when the top's up. The temperature was plummeting, and I shivered as I waited in the parking lot for Jonah to make his escape. The weather report came on the radio, and I wasn't too pleased to hear the meteorologist predicting an ice storm later that night. The last thing I needed was a lupine Ice Capades on my hands. Especially since I couldn't skate.

Jonah opened the school doors and dashed out, hunched against the wind. It took him a minute to see me; I'd parked behind Kiki's Escalade because I figured I'd be less obvious that way.

"Man, it's cold." Jonah sat down in the passenger seat and rubbed his hands together.

"You're very observant." I pulled out of the parking lot, trying to drive casually. Which is harder than it sounds.

My brother finally looked at my face and recoiled so hard that he smacked his head on the headrest. "Holy crap, Kate! What the hell happened to you?"

"Bryan wolfed out and threw me into a wall." I glanced at my face in the rearview mirror and immediately wished I hadn't. I looked like I'd given myself a Brillo pad facial. Contusions ran along the length of my cheek, which was a nice rosy purple. A huge knot decorated the right side of my forehead. I was growing horns. Or one horn, anyway. I sighed. "So you were right after all. Come on; I know you're dying to rub it in."

Instead of whipping a smart-ass crack back at me, he turned the heater up to max and directed the blowers right at me. I looked that bad.

"Here," he said. "So you don't freeze."

"Thanks."

"Any chance you'll let me drive?"

"Just give me one more minute behind the wheel before my eyes swell shut, okay? You can drive us back."

I expected him to argue, but he only shrugged. "No biggie. Gives me a chance to arm myself."

"I don't think pseudoswords will do much against were-wolves, Jonah. You have no idea how strong they are."

"I'm not talking about swords." He reached into the minus-cule storage space behind the seats and retrieved a plastic bag from Country Market. Its contents clanked and clattered.

"What's that?" I asked.

"Silverware. I didn't have time to melt it into bullets, but I figured we could pelt the fiend with it if we had to."

"Jonah," I said, "I don't understand how you can say things like that and still have loads of girls following you around."

"Honestly?" He produced a butter knife and tested the edge with his thumb. "Me either."

I'd turned into a nervous wreck by the time we reached Nano-tech Industries. Because really, what was I going to do? Stalk in and publicly accuse Sebastian of stealing a nanomachine that makes people hairy, magnetic, and highly violent? I had a wack-job reputation already; I didn't need to make it worse.

The front doors were covered in that silver reflective stuff that makes it impossible to see inside. I stared at myself in the reflection, Jonah hovering protectively at my elbow.

"What's up?" he asked.

"Just a case of nerves." I shrugged as if I could physically shake off the feeling. Which only made me feel stupider.

As my younger brother, Jonah had every right to make fun of me for that, but he didn't. All he said was, "I've got your back."

We'd faced down zombies and lived to tell the tale. Repeatedly. To various news agencies. So I felt reassured by his presence. I didn't say that out loud, though, because this wasn't a Hallmark movie. Thank god.

He followed me inside, and we made it about five steps in before stopping to gape. The reception area looked like something out of a sci-fi movie; everything was silver, white, and uncomfortable-looking. Flat screens ringed the walls, showing a series of constantly morphing pictures: rain forest to frog, frog to human, human to wolf, wolf to rock, rock to car, and so on. As I watched, a test tube full of blood morphed into a silver and red magnet. Probably a coincidence.

I didn't believe that, of course. Especially when I realized that maybe this wasn't Sebastian running off half-cocked on his own. Maybe the people at Nanotech had nanobotted him on purpose. I didn't like that thought one bit.

"Nanotech Industries, how can I help you?" a seemingly genderless person sitting behind a desk-shaped piece of glass asked us in a monotone.

"We're here to see Sebastian Black, please," I said, trying not to sound as freaked out as I was. "He's one of your interns? It's important."

"Your name?" It arched a brow at me. It was plumpish, short-haired, and smooth-faced—probably a clone. I knew I'd better not make it angry, or machine guns would pop out of its arms and we'd all be toast. Bullet-riddled toast.

"Kate Grable."

It came out calmly, like freaky clone-type people were nothing to run shrieking from. And it must have worked, because the clone pushed a few buttons on its keyboard, muttered to itself, and said, "Just a minute. You can wait over there."

It gestured to a bank of unsteady-looking stools. They were so narrow that I couldn't imagine sitting on one, but I walked toward them because I figured throwing them might make for a handy distraction in the event that things went bad. Jonah sat on one, or tried to, anyway. It tipped every time he tried to take his feet off the floor.

"This place gives me the creeps," he muttered.

"Join the club."

A guy who looked remarkably normal approached us. He was balding and portly, with horn-rimmed glasses and a lab coat. Total stereotypical lab geek. He was probably an automaton.

"I'm Terry," he said in a totally unexpected Vaderish bass. He took one look at my face and then flicked his eyes away like if he looked too long, the bruises might be catching. "How can I help you?"

"Actually, we're waiting for Sebastian. Sebastian Black?"

"Sebastian isn't in today. Can I help you with something?"

"Um . . ." I thought fast. "I work with him at the ME's office. I just needed to talk to him about some work-related stuff. There's a report my boss wanted, and I can't finish it without Sebastian's help."

"Sorry, miss. I'm afraid I can't help you."

"Damn it." Now that I'd started, the lies just rolled off my tongue. "My boss is going to sentence me to an eternity cleaning out the cold room. Do you know where I could find him? The ME really wants that report right away."

If this whole doctor thing didn't work out, I probably had a future in acting. I wasn't a doctor; I just played one in my imagination.

"I wish I did, honey," he said. "He was supposed to be here this afternoon, but he hasn't shown up in two days. I called his house and left messages, but no luck. If you manage to hunt him down, could you have him call me? I'm in pretty much the same boat you are; management is going to have my head on a platter if I don't get in touch with him."

"I'd try to hunt him down at home, but I don't have his address. Do you?"

"Sorry. I can't give out that kind of information. Not without getting fired."

"Yeah." I sighed. "I understand, but you can't blame me for trying. Mind if I leave my number in case he shows up? And I could have him call you if I find him."

"It's a deal."

We exchanged contact information. When he handed me his card, our fingers brushed. His were cold and waxy. I didn't want to contemplate the possible explanations for that. I snatched the paper away and practically ran for the door.

I wanted antibac gel. Badly. It probably wouldn't deactivate nanobots, but it was the best I could do. Jonah must have felt the same way, because we practically raced each other to the parking lot.

He saw the car first. He'd pulled ahead in the mad dash for automotive safety, and I ran into his back when he stopped in shock. I twisted my ankle and nearly fell, which didn't exactly make me happy.

"What the heck are you doing?" I snapped.

Then I saw what he was looking at. His cute little sports car was covered in gore. Red streaks smeared the windows, dripping with gobs of material I couldn't identify and didn't want to. Bits of fluff and half-decayed leaves stuck to the glistening streaks of blood. Across the hood, jagged letters spelled GO A-WAY.

Jonah looked like he wanted to cry. I couldn't decide whether to throw up or make snarky comments about Sebastian's use of random hyphens, because who else could it be? Then I realized that he was probably close by. Probably watching us. I crouched to look under the car. Nothing. Craned my neck to check the vacant lot next door. More nothing. It didn't make me feel much better.

"Is that . . ." Jonah gulped. "Is that human blood?"

I moved closer, looking at the clumps of flesh strewn all over the car. "I don't think so. It looks like an animal to me. There's bits of fur all over. . . ."

"Well, how am I supposed to get it off my car?" he wailed.

"I'd suggest washing it before it freezes on there, you idiot." It wasn't my most sympathetic moment, but I couldn't help myself. My car had once been covered in zombie puke, and you hadn't seen me crying like a little girl over it. Funny how Jonah could man up in the face of outside threats but turned into a total wuss whenever we were alone.

"But how will I see to get to the car wash?"

"Have you heard of this handy new invention? It's called a windshield wiper. Turn them on and let's go."

I opened the door with one finger, careful not to get any of the yuck on me. From inside, the car looked like a bordello, all the light tinted red. And now I really needed antibac wipes. Too bad the container in Jonah's glove compartment was totally empty.

CHAPTER
sixteen

We had to take the car through the wash twice before all the goop came off. The windows were still a little pink-tinged afterward, but it would have to do. We were wasting time, and I didn't like that. Not when Sebastian was on the loose. He had some serious explaining to do. I was so not cool with his wolfing out and killing people.

After we'd gotten the car cleaned, Jonah went to his computer lair to try to track down Sebastian's address. I decided it was time to warn Rocky since school was almost out. I didn't want her to go to the hospital for a visit, discover that Bryan was missing, and totally panic. Or even worse, run into him and get hurt.

She had independent voice study this period, and I knew sometimes she kept her phone in the booth with her while she practiced. So I texted her and waited impatiently, drumming my fingers on the table. I wasn't being unreasonable. Rocky was known for her speedy text replies. Sometimes I honestly suspected she might be a cyborg; I didn't understand how else she could text so fast.

After fifteen minutes with no response, I dialed her number with shaking hands. At this point, any delay was cause for panic.

The call went to voice mail.

Now I was flipping out. Experience had taught me that when Rocky doesn't answer me, bad things are happening. Or she was in the shower, but I was pretty sure that wasn't the case today.

Still, I couldn't panic just yet. Maybe she was actually singing during vocal study. Her voice could crack glass, so it wouldn't surprise me if she didn't hear the phone. I dialed again.

"Bayview Senior High, this is Phyllis."

"Good afternoon, Phyllis." I tried to pitch my voice a little lower so I might actually sound mature. I ended up sounding more like I had a bad head cold. "This is Amy from the Intensive Care Unit at Bayview Hospital. I urgently need to speak to Roxanne Micucci. Can you help me?"

"Oh, is this about her boyfriend?" Phyllis asked. "He was one of our office helpers as a student; I hope he's okay."

"Yes, it is. But there's no need to panic." I tried to sound soothing and actually croaked instead. Like bullfrog croaked.

"Well, I'm sorry to tell you this, but Roxanne didn't show up today. I assumed she was at the hospital, but we hadn't gotten a call. I never thought of her as the type who would skip. Strange."

"Rocky would—" The words came out in my normal voice,

and I hurriedly forced a cough to cover it up. "She was here a while ago; perhaps she went home to sleep. Thanks so much for your time."

"You're welcome, Amy, and—"

I hung up on her. When I put my phone down, it rattled against the table. I was shaking that hard.

"Jonah!" I ran to the basement door and stuck my head down the stairs. "Are you done yet?"

"Quit rushing me!" he yelled. "Be patient, damn it!"

"I'm going to look for Rocky. She's missing."

"Hurry back. I'm hoping to be done in the next half hour or so."

"Gotcha."

"Oh, and Kate?" I paused to listen. "Don't get eaten."

My brother could be such a bastard sometimes.

Back at the hospital yet again, I checked the lobby. No Rocky, although I did attract a lot of attention from the woman behind the information desk. She looked like she was about to pee herself, and at first I couldn't figure out what was wrong with her. Then I realized I was puffy-faced, bruised, still vaguely bluish, and muttering to myself. She probably thought . . . well, I had no idea what she thought, because there wasn't any rational explanation that would account for my appearance.

I was heading for the cafeteria when I realized I was going about this all wrong. I approached the lady at the desk and tried to calm her with a smile, but the whole right side of my face had gradually swollen up over the past half hour or so. I was certain that I looked like Frankenstein's geeky younger sister. From her expression, she expected me to try to eat her.

"I've lost my friend," I said as clearly as I could manage. "Can you page her for me?"

"I'm sorry," she squeaked, practically cowering behind the desk. "We're not allowed to page visitors."

It was so tempting to explain to her that I wasn't a psychotic killer like some people I knew, and that my dilapidated appearance was the result of a face-first encounter with a wall, but I didn't think it would do any good. With my luck, I'd end up getting myself thrown out of the hospital again, so I just walked away.

I took a detour through the cafeteria, and there was Rocky, watching some random talk show and eating pudding. I probably would have yelled at her for scaring me if I hadn't been so happy to see her. Evidently, she didn't share the sentiment. I ran toward her with my arms outstretched, because after all that had happened I could have really used a hug. She took one look at me and shrieked.

"Kate!" she exclaimed. "Oh my god! What happened?"

"Don't you know?" I grabbed her spoon and took a bite. Vanilla. "What happened to you? I nearly had a cardiovascular event when I tried to find you at school and they said you hadn't called in."

"Oh." She blinked. "I must have forgotten to ask my mom to call. What day is it again?"

I let out a long, slow breath and tried to resist the urge to throttle her. "Have you seen Bryan lately?"

"They took him for more tests a couple of hours ago, so I went home to take a shower. I was just on my way to grab a coffee and head back up. Why?" she said, her voice rising. "Is there something wrong? What happened to your face? Why are you blue?"

"Well," I said, "Bryan's gone." She screeched again, throwing up her hands and flinging pudding all over the place. I tried to dodge the droplets, but I had about as much luck as I'd had dodging Bryan's whatever-he-hit-me-with.

"Gone?" she said. "What do you mean, gone? Like . . . he's dead?"

She dissolved into tears, dropping her face into her hands. Yep, now I felt like an insensitive ass.

"No!" I grabbed her by the shoulders, forcing her to look at me. "Gone as in got up and left the hospital. He's fine. Ish."

My lips twitched. I couldn't keep them under control, because I was such a horrible liar. But Rocky wasn't looking at me, not really. She was having a hard time focusing through the tears.

"So he's okay?" She took in a hitching breath, and then her voice hardened. "He left without me?"

"It's not his fault. He's . . ." I didn't want to say this out loud, but Rocky of all people deserved to know what was going on. "I think he's got nanobots."

"Nanobots?"

"Teeny little robots. They make him very strong, and very

fast and very . . . uh . . . hairy. I know how crazy it sounds, but I'm pretty sure I'm right. Did he have any superfluous hair when you left the room?"

"Superfluous what?" She took a deep, calming breath. "He looked normal to me."

"Well, then there are a few things you need to know." I tried to wipe the pudding off my shirt and just succeeded in smearing it around. "He grew a bunch of extra hair. Fur, really. Like, all over his body."

"So he's like a werewolf?"

"Kind of, but not exactly. I think if we can get rid of the bots, he'll be back to normal."

"He can't be a werewolf!"

"It'll be okay, Rock. I'm sure we can help him; I've just got to figure out how."

"You don't understand," she wailed. "I'm Team Edward!"

CHAPTER
seventeen

Rocky and I sat idling in my driveway for two whole minutes before I got impatient. Still no Jonah. I honked the horn, long and loud. He probably couldn't even hear it down in the basement. If he was flirting with one of his groupies in the Roargan Kross chat rooms, I was going to duct-tape him to a chair and let the werewolves have him.

I dialed the house, but he didn't answer. Then I tried his cell.

"Did he pick up?" Rocky was as tense as I was. She gnawed on a fingernail, even though there was nothing left for her to chew.

"Voice mail." My voice came out terse.

Now I was a little scared, and that made me mad. If he was just dorking around with me, I'd kill him with my bare hands. I stomped to the front door, prepared to yell. Practical jokes were fine in nonemergency situations; I'd played a few on him myself.

Part of the whole sibling deal. But scaring me for real? Totally uncool.

My feet crunched through the snow Jonah was supposed to shovel but hadn't because he'd been too busy geeking it up. I'd left my boots at home, and snow got into my socks. As if I wasn't pissed enough already.

The front door stood halfway open, and I opened my mouth to yell at my stupid brother for letting all the heat out, when I noticed the splintered remains of the jamb. It looked like someone had kicked the door in.

The panic hit me so hard it honestly hurt. My chest constricted, the muscles knotting themselves into little knots of holy crap. I croaked his name. No answer. Not surprised.

Rocky came up the walk behind me, casual and unaware. I shooed her away without looking at her, because I didn't want something to sneak up on me and use me as a chew toy.

"Go call Detective Despain," I said quietly. "And lock yourself in the car."

"But . . ." She started to back away even as she protested.

"Now."

She ran off.

I entered the house alone. Better that way, really. I didn't have to worry about Rocky now, and I needed all my wits about me. They were the only real weapon I had.

The foyer was empty except for a piece of mail on the floor. I picked it up automatically and almost put it into the wicker mail bin so it wouldn't get lost. But then I realized it wasn't mail at all. It was Sebastian's address, scrawled across the back of an envelope in Jonah's cockeyed handwriting. I put it in my pocket.

Something crashed downstairs, so loud it shook the floorboards beneath my feet. It took me about a half a second to get to the basement, or at least that was what it felt like. I'd never run so fast before.

Jonah was belly-down on the puke-colored practice mats.

I lunged forward, tripped over my own foot, and skidded to a stop next to my brother's motionless body. When I flipped him over, the first thing I noticed was a syringe waggling obscenely from the skin of his neck. The plunger wasn't pressed; I pulled it out of his neck before I accidentally injected him with whatever mystery substance was inside.

Someone hit me from behind. My teeth clicked together, and my jaw slammed against the floor as I went down. The pain was huge. My attacker leapt onto me, pressing my body into the mats with his weight. I felt his panting breath, hot on my cheek. I tried to heave him off, but he shoved his hips forward, pinning me more securely. It became a struggle to breathe. Black spots danced behind my eyes.

I was going to die. Or maybe something worse.

He snatched the syringe from my hand. Moments later, my neck stung as he jabbed it with the needle. I whipped my head back and forth and shrieked, as if that were going to do any good.

He grabbed my head and ground my cheek into the floor. I could see him in my peripheral vision, or his hair, anyway. It was long and blond and covered most of his bulging, distorted face.

At least I knew it wasn't Bryan; he had brown hair. That would have really capped off the suck.

Sebastian was blond, though. I couldn't be sure it was him without a better look, but it was the only logical conclusion.

"Welcome to the pack," he growled.

His voice was rough and completely unrecognizable. I almost tried to reason with him, because it seemed like the thing to do. Like maybe if I could appeal to his logic, he'd get up and administer the antidote, and everything would be rainbows and fuzzy bunnies. But then I noticed a bunch of glass on the floor, spilling out the door of my laboratory.

I let out another shriek, but this time it was anger and not fear. I couldn't see much, because my glasses were falling off and my distance vision wasn't so great without them. But I could figure it out. That crash? All the contents of my workbench shattering because that hairy bastard had flipped it over.

I bucked once, as hard as I could. My legs pistoned out and my body rocketed off the floor. This time, he didn't expect it. He didn't go flying or anything, but he did release me. I fully expected him to pounce again, but he didn't. He fled instead, sprinting up the stairs so fast I could barely track the movement.

It wasn't smart to follow him, not without a way to cure or contain him. And I had to help my brother. I checked for a pulse. Thank god, he was alive, and respirating too. I quickly discovered a contusion on the back of his head; he'd been hit pretty hard. His eyelids fluttered when I touched the injury. He'd be conscious again soon, and probably regretting every second.

"Rocky," I murmured.

I knew she had enough common sense not to confront an enraged werewolf, so I wasn't too worried. Not about her. I was worried about Jonah, and what those nanobots were doing to me right now, and the fact that I was probably way over my daytime minutes and my parents were going to kill me. But not so much about Rocky.

Not until I got upstairs and saw the empty driveway. She was gone.

CHAPTER
eighteen

I ran to the end of the street, heavy breaths steaming the air. Rocky wasn't anywhere in sight, so I called her. Someone picked up the phone for about two seconds. Just long enough for me to hear her yelling in the background.

"Let me go, you freak!"

Then it went dead. I called again and got voice mail.

I needed to tell Despain everything. My best friend had probably been kidnapped by a nanobotted boy with werewolf tendencies. Who knew where he'd gone? Or what he planned to do to her? The police needed to be involved, and Despain was one of the best detectives I'd met. And I'd met a lot.

I dialed her number and she answered after half a ring. "What's up, Kate?"

"Someone just attacked my brother in our basement. We need help."

"I'll get an ambulance there right away. Where are you now?"

"In the driveway."

"I'll be there in a minute."

"Thank you." I paused on my way back to the house. "And Despain?"

"What?"

I'd intended to tell her about my Sebastian-related suspicions, but now I was having second thoughts. If she tried to arrest him, he'd probably kill her, too. And let's say she got lucky and shot him. What if he was the only one who knew how to deactivate the nanobots? I'd be doomed to a life of superfluous hair and locked cages. No med school. No anything. I could deal with the hair, but the thought of losing control of my mind terrified me.

My best choice was to track him down, save Rocky, and make him tell me how to de-wolf myself. I probably had an hour or two before I started wolfing out.

Sebastian had welcomed me to the pack. I was going to take that welcome and shove it down his hairy throat.

"Nothing," I said. "Just come quick, okay?"

The only answer was a click.

I had just a couple of minutes until she'd show up. Jonah's car was gone. Mom and Dad were at a bed and breakfast for the night. It was only an hour away, but right now that felt like an eternity. The only car in the garage was my old, cruddy sedan. The crapmobile.

I sped away, breaking about five laws in the process. I didn't care. My best friend was in danger. Heck, I didn't even stop to put on my seat belt.

Sebastian's address was the only lead I had, so that was where I started searching. The house was one of those borderline mansions with a pair of stone lions flanking the driveway. I'd always thought the concept of a stone lion as a status symbol was completely ridiculous. I mean, really. Nothing says success like a huge cat made out of concrete.

I trotted up the driveway, staying alert for any signs of movement on the grounds so I didn't get surprised again. Now that I was here, I felt like a total idiot. Why hadn't I gotten the silverware out of Jonah's car? I had nothing to protect myself with, and I needed to remedy that fast. When I searched my pockets, all I found was a lone mitten, a pocket pharmaceutical guide, and a spork. I had no idea how the spork had gotten in there and no hope that it would withstand a werewolf attack, but holding it made me feel marginally better.

I rang the bell, looking over my shoulder with paranoia. I was ready for anything except for the trophy wife who opened the door. She was scary tan, obviously surgically enhanced, and had glossy black bangs that hung over her eyes, almost completely obscuring her vision.

When I recovered from the shock, I said, "I'm looking for Sebastian, please."

"Huh?" She looked genuinely confused.

"Sebastian? I need to see him. Now." I made a mental note to not use any big words and strain the few brain cells she had left.

"You're blue."

I took a deep, calming breath. "I know."

"Upstairs."

She jerked her thumb toward the stairs, like I needed to be instructed on how to get from the first floor to the second. Then again, idiocy was probably common in her usual social circle, so I tried not to take offense. I stepped into a foyer as large as the first floor of my house, complete with a fountain full of koi.

The trophy wife jiggled back down the hall to whatever cavernous depths she had come from. Once she was gone, I went upstairs and was faced with a long hallway with a row of identical white doors on either side, all of which were closed. I figured I might as well start with the ones closest to the stairs, because I didn't want to get boxed in by a werewolf. I felt pretty impressed with myself for thinking of that. I hadn't spent all that time listening to Jonah play DORK, aka Dragons of Roargan Kross, for nothing; apparently, I'd picked up some battle tactics along the way.

Of course, this meant I was a bigger dork than I thought.

I took a deep breath and flung the first door open. A millisecond after I committed to this course of action, I realized I could be barging into Sebastian's bedroom. If I was wrong, if Rocky had been coincidentally kidnapped by a different werewolf altogether, this could be bad. I could accidentally walk in on him in his underwear. I'd need therapy for the rest of my life.

Luckily, the room turned out to be a guest room. A nauseatingly frilly one.

I shut the door on Frillville and moved down the hall. This time, I knocked first. I figured I had a better chance of keeping Sebastian calm if I didn't embarrass him by barging in. If I could keep him from wolfing out, maybe we could settle this without a fight.

Behind the second door was a bedroom that had obviously been a guy's at one time, so I entered cautiously. It was uninhabited except for the hordes of scantily clad bikini models staring at me from the walls. And the ceiling. I had the intense urge to get a Sharpie and draw mustaches on them, but I didn't.

The final door on this side of the hall. No answer to my knock. But when I cracked it open, I immediately knew I'd found the right place. I could sense the geekiness before I could even see inside. It smelled like stale Mountain Dew. I pushed the door open the rest of the way, and it was like walking into my own room, only done in darker colors and about twice the size. There were books and papers strewn across every available surface. On the desk beside the door sat a copy of my favorite anatomy book, balanced precariously atop a rack of test-tube-shaped lights, and I automatically moved it. Fire hazard. Besides, that book was too good to go up in smoke.

I didn't see Sebastian or Rocky. It was probably too much to hope that he'd be sitting on the bed, waiting for me to show up so he could surrender and return my best friend safe and sound.

"Sebastian?" I called, pitching my voice low.

There were two doors on the left-hand wall. I arbitrarily picked the one on the left. But by this time, I was sick of the whole door-opening production. I didn't exactly fling it open, but I didn't knock, either.

It was a bathroom. Sebastian stood in front of the foggy mirror in his underwear, shaving. When I barged in, he immediately sliced his cheek open.

"Ow!" he yelled, clapping his hand to the cut.

"Superfluous hair!" I shouted, pointing at him. "I knew it!"

He didn't seem to know where to put his hands. One was on his cheek, staunching the blood. The other hovered between his tighty-whities and his concave chest, trying to cover them both but completely failing. Finally he grabbed a towel, smearing blood all over the pristine white cotton, and wrapped it around himself.

"What are you doing here?" he demanded.

"Where's my best friend, you bastard?" I shot back.

"Who?"

He only looked confused. I could sympathize; I was a little foozled myself. I'd expected him to go all werebotty, but he was mousy, as usual. Maybe his bots were broken.

"You abducted my best friend from my house. Or don't you remember?" I said.

"What? I don't— What are you talking about?" he sputtered.

"Give me your hand. I want to see something."

He held out his hand automatically. I bet I could have gotten him to jump up and down on one leg and make chicken noises if I'd wanted. He was just that spineless. I found it increasingly more difficult to picture him as any kind of killer, even an accidental one.

I didn't see any signs of abnormal hair growth, but he had fine white-blond hair, so it was hard to tell. He snatched his hand back before I could feel for stubble.

"Well?" he asked, growing a spine at the most inopportune time. "Are you satisfied now? Because I'd like you to go so I can put some pants on."

"I . . . you can't . . ." I couldn't stop stammering. I tell him my friend got abducted, and he's concerned about his pants? I didn't understand what the heck was going on in his head, so I went on the offensive. "I'll go as soon as you tell me what's up with the nanobots."

"How did you—the—what? I don't know what you're talking about."

It wasn't the most convincing act I'd ever seen.

"Nanobots." I enunciated the word carefully. "I know you have them, and I know they got Holly killed. And the other guy—that's her brother, right? And now my friend got taken by someone affected by the bots. So you can either spill the whole story or I'm telling the police. By the way, my friends know where I am, so getting rid of me isn't going to help your situation."

Yeah, that last bit was a blatant lie, but he didn't even seem to notice. Apparently, I was better at lying to werewolves than I was to my parents. Not like I tried to lie to them often, but it happened from time to time.

"You're crazy," he said.

"No, I'm not."

He didn't respond, so I pressed my advantage. I got right up in his face, even if it did put me uncomfortably close to his underwear. I had no time for prissiness.

Although I reserved the right to barf retroactively.

"How exactly did it go?" I asked, pinning him with my eyes. "You got sick of all the jocks picking on you and figured you'd show them for once? So you injected yourself with untested nanobots. That's not smart, dude, and you know that. The potential side effects are staggering. I mean, you've seen Spider-Man, right? You should damn well know better."

"That's not how it went at all," he said, but he couldn't meet my eyes.

"Yeah?" I snorted. "Then why are you shaving off all the hair?"

"I don't know what you're talking about."

"The hair, you idiot. The nanos cause extreme hypertrichosis."

I grabbed his arm and yanked it toward me. Unfortunately, said arm was holding up the towel, which slithered to the floor too quickly for him to grab. I had proof. I wasn't letting it go, even if it was wearing uncomfortably tight underwear.

"See, you're shaving it off. . . ."

But then I stopped. His arm had a smattering of fine blond hairs on it. No stubble. Nothing like the furry stuff I'd pulled out of Bryan or the samples I'd taken from the scene of the attack. Not at all.

Was I actually wrong about something science-related? The

thought made me all shaky and breathless, like the girl in a vampire romance. I sank down to a squat and tried not to flip out, because then I would have to stage an intervention on myself.

I'd thought I was over all those worries about my potential hackness once I'd defeated the zombies, but they all came flooding back. Because really, what did I know? I'd cured Grable's disease, true, but that didn't exactly make me the high school equivalent of Alexander Fleming. I was back to hackdom again; you'd think I would have been used to it by now.

The bath mat I crouched on was an ugly tan color, at odds with the rampant lacy crapness infesting the rest of the house. The bathroom itself burgeoned with pink lace: the curtains on the window, the rose-printed soap holder, even the frill-covered tissue box. It was an anomaly, this bath mat, but I couldn't get my hacky brain to make sense of it.

"Kate?" Sebastian folded his arms and looked at me with a stern expression. "Are you on drugs?"

I looked up at him, and that simple head motion threw my crouch entirely off balance. I put one hand down to steady myself. The bath mat felt coarse underneath my fingers, and I jerked instinctively away from its yucky crunchiness. Something stuck to my fingers, and I whipped them around wildly trying to get it off, like maybe it was infective or something. Tufts of tan fluff scattered across the floor; I could see a pile of it under the vanity.

That bath mat was covered entirely with hair. And I'd just touched it.

I leapt off the mat, shoved an increasingly bewildered Sebastian out of the way, and washed my hands. Twice. In scalding water. Not that I thought the hair was going to do anything to me, but I didn't exactly know what part of Sebastian's body this hair came from.

"What the heck is wrong with you?" he asked, picking the towel up and wrapping it around himself again. I noticed bits of hair stuck to the towel, but I didn't mention them because he might drop it again, and my overstressed psyche couldn't take much more of that.

"Sebastian?" I tried to sound all logical and not entirely grossed out. "If you don't know what I'm talking about, why do you have a bath mat covered in human hair?"

CHAPTER
nineteen

Sebastian and I stood in his bathroom. Actually, that's not quite descriptive enough. We glared at each other over a hairy bath mat, and he was wearing only a pair of undies and a towel. It wasn't exactly the kind of situation I expected to find myself in when I'd gotten out of bed that morning.

"I don't know what you're talking about," he said, but we both knew he was lying.

"This!" I waved my hand, which despite the vigorous washing still had little strands of hair stuck to it. "The hair. On your bath mat. The nanos stimulate hair growth, don't they? One of my friends turned into a werewolf and threw me into a wall yesterday. Rocky is missing. So I do not have any patience left. You better start talking right now, damn it, or I'm calling the cops."

His shoulders slumped at the mere mention of the police.

The towel slumped too, but I kept my eyes glued firmly to his face.

"All right," he said. "All right. But it's not what you think."

"Of course it isn't. You injected yourself with untested nano-machines by accident. Whoops."

I was awfully proud at the amount of sarcasm I managed to pack into those few words, but he didn't even seem to notice. Un-appreciated again.

"I didn't use the nanobots on myself. I was going to, but my girlfriend talked some sense into me first." He met my eyes for the first time since I'd burst into his bathroom. "You've got to believe me. I'll admit that I took them from Nanotech; I thought maybe it would change things. Look at me. I'm twenty-two and I still live with my parents. My only social interaction is on *Roargan Kross*. I'm tired of being a nerd. You know what I mean."

I resented the implication that I was somewhere in his league. "Actually, Sebastian, I have no freaking clue." I scowled, but I didn't yell because I remembered all too well what a wuss he was. He'd devolve into a quivering blob of primordial jelly, which would be cool to experiment on but not so helpful when it came to extracting information on the nanobot front. "But go on. I assume Holly was your girlfriend?"

He nodded, and his face started to scrunch up in what I'd begun to recognize as his pre-breakdown expression. I quickly changed the subject. "Okay. So you stole the nanobots from work. And then what happened?"

"My brother took them. I was in here with the syringe, trying to get up the courage to use them on myself, but Holly talked me out of it. I decided to return them to work so no one would ever know they were gone in the first place. But my brother overheard us. His bedroom's right next to mine. He took the bots from me by force and used them on himself."

"He sounds like a great guy," I said.

"I didn't know what to do. But nothing happened right away, and I started hoping they hadn't worked. We'd never used them on humans, you know. But the next morning, he came in and threw me into the wall." He paused, rubbing his head.

"I feel your pain. Trust me."

"He came home from school early, ranting about throwing encyclopedias. I would have thought he was hallucinating except that he'd miraculously grown fur; it was still growing so fast that I literally watched it get longer. He wanted to know about the bots, kept rambling about how great he felt and how strong he was. And he kept talking about recruiting, like he was some kind of supervillain or something. He held me up by the throat, and I couldn't breathe. So I told him everything."

"What do you mean, everything?"

"I'll give you the documentation so you can read for yourself. The nanobots enhance muscular response, making people faster and stronger. He was particularly interested to know that they're bloodborne."

I snorted. "Of course. He wants to start his own pack. I take it he's a Twi-hard?"

"A what?"

"Never mind. Go on."

"Then Holly's brother Herbie came into town to visit, and we were hanging out at the coffee shop one night while Holly was working. My brother showed up and started pushing me around, and Herbie threatened to call the cops. My brother just snapped, and he tore Herbie apart with his bare hands. I saw it; I was right there, and I guess I dropped Dr. Burr's ID when I ran. He's always leaving it places, and I'd found it on the floor on my way out of work and meant to give it back to him.

"Anyway. You have no idea how scared I was. I came back here and locked myself in my room. Holly didn't know anything, but my brother was convinced that she was going to turn him in. He was in here ranting and raving about it. I think the bots are making him paranoid. And then he killed her too. I know he did."

He broke off, his lower lip quivering. Part of me felt bad for him, but mostly I wanted to spin him around and check for a spine. There had to be one in there somewhere.

"So why not go to the police?" I asked.

He gave me a don't-be-an-idiot look, which under the circumstances was the most insulting thing he could have possibly done. I wasn't the one who stole potentially dangerous nanomaterials. And then there was the part where he was voluntarily standing on a bath mat covered in his brother's hair. That went beyond stupidity and into psychosis territory.

"Isn't that obvious?" he asked. "I don't want to die too."

"All right," I said. "Let's say that I believe you. What do you plan to do about it?"

"Do?" His eyes widened. "I'll tell you what I'm doing: I'm installing three dead bolts on my bedroom door, and I've got food supplies stashed under my bed. I'm locking myself in until he burns out. It's got to happen sometime; his body's on metabolic overload. The bots are hypersensitive to adrenaline; we found out in the animal testing. The more he produces, the quicker he'll burn out. So all I've got to do is wait."

"And then what? He dies?"

Sebastian shrugged uncomfortably. "Anything's possible."

I stood there for a minute, thinking hard. Or trying to, anyway. The bare-chestedness was really distracting. "Do us both a favor and put on some clothes, will you?"

He looked down, like somehow he'd forgotten the fact that he was standing there in his undies. I didn't know how; I certainly hadn't been able to forget it. He wiped the dried blood off his face and put on some pants. A shirt would have been nice, but I wasn't about to ask for miracles.

After he got dressed, he turned to me for further instructions. I was ready.

"First, I need that documentation you mentioned before."

He handed over a heavy notebook bound with a pink plastic spiral. "If somebody catches you with this, I'm going to be in big trouble. That's proprietary information, you know."

I glared at him. "If someone catches me, this binder will be the least of your troubles. You understand?"

"Yes." He hung his head.

"All right. Do you have any idea where I can find your brother?"

"I don't know. I haven't seen him since yesterday."

"Well, you're no help," I said. "I'm going now. If you see your brother, call me."

I rummaged through the junk on his desk without bothering to ask first, because he didn't have the spine to say no to anything as far as I could tell. Finally, I found a pen. I scribbled my number on the back of an envelope and tacked it to his wall, where he couldn't lose it without really making an effort.

Something was bothering me. I couldn't put my finger on it, but I had the feeling that I was missing something important, like a mental itch I couldn't quite reach. It wasn't like I didn't have a lot on my mind. Rocky was still missing, and Bryan was a werewolf, and Jonah probably had a concussion, and my relationship with Aaron was possibly over, and I had to figure out how to deactivate the nanobots without killing anybody, especially myself. And if that wasn't enough, I was officially late for Rockathon setup. Kiki was probably going to throttle me if someone else didn't get there first.

Wait a minute. Rockathon. The chairs. I got out the sheet of paper Kiki had given me.

"Sebastian, what's your address?"

"Seventeen Meadowbrook Lane."

I thought I might throw up. The paper in my hand said:

```
Trey Black, 17 Meadowbrook Lane
```

"Your brother is Trey Black?"

"Yeah." He took one look at my stricken expression and stepped away like I might hit him. "What? Do you know Trey?"

"I know him." I had the intense urge to put my head in my hands and stay there for about a hundred years. But someone would eventually find me in Sebastian's bedroom, which would give a whole new definition to the word *humiliating*.

"Yeah, you would. You go to Bayview, right? Are you friends or something?"

"Hardly." I took the binder and forced my feet to move toward the door. "He keeps trying to put the moves on me despite the fact that he's friends with my boyfriend. I honestly don't get it."

"That sounds like my brother. When we lived in Honolulu, he stole my prom date. After we got to prom."

"Wow. And I thought I had it bad."

He nodded mournfully. "They took off in the limo together. I saved up for months to rent that limo. But that's just how he rolls. He honestly couldn't give a crap what anybody else thinks. When he sees something he wants, he hunts it down and kills it."

"Excuse me. He seems to want *me* right now."

I glared at him so hard he actually whimpered. It didn't make me feel better. Nothing would make me feel better now that I knew the king werewolf was my boyfriend's new best friend.

Of course, Aaron probably wasn't my boyfriend anymore. Somehow, that failed to make me feel better too.

* * *

A few minutes later, I let myself out the front door, cradling the binder like it contained the Ten freaking Commandments. The trophy wife stood in the driveway next to my car with a camera in one hand and a flyswatter in the other.

"Um," I said. "What are you doing?"

"I think there's a Yeti in our yard." She sounded half terrified, half thrilled. Under the seven pounds of makeup, her eyes were wide. "I'm going to make millions off the video."

A Yeti? I scanned the bushes for werewolves. No luck. So I tiptoed to the stone lions and checked behind them.

"They're not real," whispered the trophy wife.

"What are you talking about?" I asked.

"The lions. They're stone. You don't need to sneak up on them."

I looked down at the stone beastie in front of me. "Yeah, I got that. I'm looking for the Yeti."

"It ran behind the house."

"Then why are you still standing here?"

"I got my video already." She shrugged. "But I thought I'd wait out here in case it came back."

"What's the flyswatter for?" I asked. She looked down at it like she wasn't sure how it had gotten into her hand. "Never mind. Look, that Yeti is my friend. I'm going to look for it. If you see him, will you yell for me?"

"Wow," she said. "You're strange."

"Thanks," I said. "But will you do it?"

She nodded, and I took off toward the side of the house.

I settled into an easy jog and then spent a moment marveling that I could ever use the word *easy* to describe a physical activity. But I'd started puffing by the time I rounded the side of the house. Sure, I could maintain an easy jog around a normal-sized home, but this was like trying to lap a football stadium with a wraparound porch. It wasn't going to happen.

It was almost a relief to find Bryan in the backyard. His face was completely distorted and borderline unrecognizable, but he was wearing the hospital gown from earlier, so I was pretty sure it was him. And the fur was the right color—dark brown, just like his hair. It wafted in the breeze as he took out a topiary shaped like an elephant. He pulled off the trunk with his bare hands and started beating the plant's hindquarters with it.

I never thought I'd see one of my friends spank an elephant with its own trunk. Heck, I never thought I'd see *anyone* do that, let alone someone I'd associate with voluntarily.

"Bryan!" I yelled. "Stop that!"

He paused, cocking his head. The gesture made me think of Armstrong. He used to give me the same questioning look when I'd tell him to do something. Apparently, Bryan's effective IQ was about equal to that of the average Labradoodle. That was good to know. Although strange, because Trey certainly didn't seem to have lost any brain cells. I'd have to think on that later.

"Put the branch down," I said firmly, pointing first at the branch and then at the ground.

Bryan looked down at the huge stick in his hand. After a moment of consideration during which I was able to fully contemplate the possibility that I could at any moment be bludgeoned, he flung it away. It whirled through the air and speared the throat of a flamingo topiary about fifty feet away. Topiaries are creepy, but I still felt kind of guilty.

"Why are you talking to me like I'm an idiot?" he asked. His voice was lower than usual, and kinda growly, but still clear enough to understand.

"Because you're an idiot."

It probably wasn't very smart to taunt the elephant spanker, but it just popped out. Luckily, all he did was chuckle. He was used to my sense of humor.

I took a couple of steps forward. "Are you okay? You're not going to throw me into a wall again, are you?"

He winced, hunching his shoulders away from me for a second like he was afraid of losing control again. So I froze. Any movement I made might send him into a hairy, nanobot-fueled haze.

We stood there for a minute.

"All right," I finally said. "I know what's wrong with you. I need you to chill while I figure out how to fix it. If you run off again, I can't help you. Can you do that for me?"

"All right," he rumbled.

I decided it was probably wise to keep Rocky's abduction a secret for now. So I led him to the car in silence.

And then he clamped his hairy hand onto my shoulder. "Where's Rocky?"

CHAPTER
twenty

"Where is Rocky?" Bryan repeated insistently, his voice deepening. I could barely understand him now. Thankfully, he released me and clamped down on one of the lawn chairs in the Black family backyard instead. The metal screeched as it bent.

I stopped and held up my hands, urging him wordlessly to settle down.

"It's okay," I said. "She's okay. Now take a deep breath. The condition you have gets worse when you get upset or scared. I need you. So does Rocky. You got me?"

After a moment, he nodded.

"Let's go to the car. You can meditate or something."

I started walking, and he followed me without any further topiary-related incidents. The trophy wife shot some video when we walked past, but we wouldn't pose for the camera the way she wanted us to. She flounced up the stairs and slammed the door on us. I was hurt by that. Really.

I got behind the wheel. Bryan sat down in the passenger seat and stared at me like I was the freak instead of the other way around. I couldn't help examining him right back. His face looked pulled out of shape, like one of those Hollywood plastic surgery addicts. His forehead bulged and his brows drew low over his eyes, giving him a serious caveman vibe. His teeth seemed too big for his mouth somehow. Of course, I couldn't see them very well under all the superfluous hair. It covered his entire face except for two bare circles around his eyes. He looked like a reverse raccoon.

"Pretty scary, huh?" he muttered.

I patted his hand. The hospital gown puffed out from all the fur crammed inside.

"You're still Bryan. Just hairier."

"I need Rocky." He squirmed uncomfortably. "Will you take me to her?"

"Of course I will!" The words came out too hastily; I had to force myself to sound casual. "But will you come with me on an errand first? I don't want to get hurt again."

"I said I was sorry." His eyes flashed, and his chest started heaving. I could almost feel his control slipping away; I wanted to open the car door and run, but that would be the worst choice I could make.

"I didn't mean you!" I said. "Really, I didn't. Trey Black beat me up. He hurt Jonah too."

Bryan snarled. But not like an angry guy. More like a pissed-off wildcat.

I took a deep breath and plunged in. "Do you think you could track Trey? Like, by scent or something? I don't know where he is, and I need to stop him from attacking anybody else. He's the one who jumped you behind the restaurant and wolfed you out."

He gritted his teeth, sinking back into the seat. On the surface, he looked relaxed. It made me feel better until I saw his hands tightly balled into fists. This was not good.

"I'll track him down," he said darkly. "Take me to the last place you saw him."

It was probably the best I'd get. Time was moving too fast, and if I didn't find a cure soon, I'd be the one throwing people into walls. Had the bots made Trey a killer, or had he always had that capacity inside him? I didn't want to find out firsthand.

I drove back to my house. Despain would probably lecture me, but once she saw Bryan I was sure she'd help us. Someone needed to figure out how to deactivate the stupid bots without killing us all, so I tried to speed-read the stupid binder when we stopped at red lights and stop signs. I figured with my luck, I'd get into an accident. With no license. Which would really suck. The whole thing gave me a headache, and I was suddenly starving on top of everything else.

I realized this wasn't the time to be complaining about the little things, especially since I had a wolfman sitting next to me wearing one of Aaron's old hoodies with the hood pulled up so he didn't scare anyone we passed. But between the building queasiness in my belly and the stabbing hunger pains, it was hard to concentrate.

My driveway was empty. A slip of paper fluttered on the front door, a couple of inches above the bloody handprint that still decorated it. I turned to reassure Bryan, because I figured he'd flip when he saw the blood, but he was asleep. The increases in strength and speed had to be consuming incredible amounts of energy, which could lead to the burnout that Sebastian mentioned. At this metabolic pace, the more energy he could conserve, the better. And letting him sleep for a few minutes gave me some time to speed-read the manual.

When I turned the car off, Bryan didn't even move. I couldn't help worrying that it was CPR time again, but then he started snoring, which was a relief until it got really annoying. I debated jabbing him with my elbow, but I couldn't bring myself to do it. I'd have to live with it.

Back to the binder. So far, I'd skimmed through a bunch of nanotech theory. While it was really interesting, it wasn't remotely helpful—although I could use it to write one killer term paper for AP Bio; I made a mental note to copy everything before I returned it. All's fair in love and Advanced Placement classes.

I flipped forward to the section on nanobot construction. Sebastian said he'd looked for some way to deactivate the bots and failed, so I wasn't exactly expecting to find an Off switch, but maybe there was some kind of weakness I could exploit. The bots were a mixture of biological and synthetic materials designed to augment physical strength and speed reflexes, which was just a fancy way of saying they were itty-bitty robots that make people as strong and fast as bears and wolves. Technically I should have called them werebearwolfbots, but that would have made me sound like a complete idiot.

Bryan started to snore at full volume, or at least I hoped it was full, because if it got much louder, my eardrums might pop.

One bit caught my eye as I read on: every test animal had died when the docs had tried to give them an MRI. The bots must have been sensitive to magnetic fields. I felt all special when the binder confirmed this. Autopsies showed that the mice had died of massive internal hemorrhaging; the bots pretty much ripped them apart.

I leaned my head back and closed my eyes, trying to find some way to make this info useful. We could put Bryan into an MRI machine to destroy the bots, but he'd die of internal bleeding. As far as side effects went, that one was about as bad as it got. I had to find some other way to interfere with the mechanical parts.

Unfortunately, I drew a blank. Hunger made it hard for me to focus. I felt so starving that I was actually dizzy. When the door opened and Aaron held his hand out to help me out of the car, I honestly thought I was hallucinating.

"You are not here," I said.

"I missed you."

When he pulled me out of the car and pressed his lips to mine, I knew what it meant. He'd chucked Elle for good this time. I smiled triumphantly against his lips, barely restraining myself from throwing my arms over my head in a display of triumph.

It probably wasn't very nice of me, but I didn't care. I wasn't obligated to be nice to wannabe boyfriend stealers. But then the smiling made it tough to kiss, so I stopped.

When we pulled apart, Aaron searched my face. "You okay?"

"Yeah. I just didn't want to leave Bryan out here by himself. How did you know we were here?"

"I didn't. I tried to call you, but your cell is off. So I came by to see if you were home."

"Stupid phone."

"So . . . ," he said, taking my hand and holding it between both of his.

I waited. It took all my willpower not to throw myself into his arms and wail about how much I had missed him. But all I needed to do was picture Elle sitting in his lap and it became much easier. I wasn't letting him off with anything short of a full apology, because he got the better deal with me. My brains would get better with age; her body wouldn't, except for maybe the synthetic boobies. I didn't think those had an expiration date, but I really wasn't sure. Synthetic boobies weren't my area of expertise.

"I'm sorry," he said. And I still waited. Because it wasn't good enough.

"I didn't mean to let it go as far as it did. I mean, yeah, I didn't want to piss her off, but it also felt good to have somebody want me that bad." He shook his head. "Stupid, I know, but you're so awesome. I mean, you're famous. The other day, I read that they might be making a TV movie about you. I'm just the quarterback of a sucky football team. How can I compete with that?"

I had nothing to say. In fact, all I could manage was a very un-attractive gape. He couldn't be feeling inferior to me. Everyone loved Aaron, and I was the class brain. That ranked me slightly above the gamer geeks in terms of coolness level, but not by much.

"Are you nuts?" I asked.

That was all I got out before a Volkswagen hopped the curb, tore up our driveway, and nearly ran me over.

CHAPTER
twenty-one

One minute, I was standing in my driveway with Aaron. The next, Elle nearly rammed me with her bumper. I scrambled to get out of the way, slipping in the slush and sprawling on the ground. Snow soaked through the seat of my jeans as the car screeched to a stop beside me.

"You," she said, flouncing out of the car. Her cheeks were red with cold, or maybe anger. I couldn't be bothered to care which.

"Your skill with pronouns is earth-shattering," I said.

I think it all would have been okay if Aaron hadn't laughed. He clamped his lips together in an attempt to stifle the noise, but it came out his nose in an explosive snort. Her face went all blotchy; patches of red competed with pale, bloodless spots for dominance. But I still couldn't resist getting just one more dig in.

"Man," I said, shaking my head in mock sympathy. "You don't look so good. Do you need an ointment or something?"

She smacked me.

My skin stung, and I knew without being told that the outline of her hand decorated my cheek. I put my hand up to it, blinking hard. I wasn't about to let her see me cry. Funny how I'd endured all kinds of pain over the past couple of days without a peep and a little slap on the face sent me over the edge.

Her eyes were wide, and she kept looking at her hand like maybe it had developed a will of its own and might strike again at any time. Then she looked at me. And she laughed.

The rush of anger was so strong that my skin tingled with it. Goose bumps rose in waves down my arms, and my fingers twitched with the urge to make fists. After all she'd done, now she was hitting me? Laughing at me? If she wanted to pick a fight, I'd show her a fight.

She must have seen something in my face that frightened her, because she tried to run. I grabbed her by the wrist and yanked before she made it very far, and her feet slipped in the slush. Her head nearly collided with the bumper on her way down to the pavement. I felt my lips pull back from my teeth and realized I was grinning.

"Kate?" The voice was unfamiliar at first, but I recognized Aaron after a moment. He looked delicious.

Elle tried to scramble away on her hands and knees, and I kicked her arms out from under her. She sprawled on her belly. Road sludge dotted her face. I laughed because it was so funny.

And when she tried to roll out of range, I followed. It wouldn't be that easy to get away from me.

"Stop it right now, Kate." Aaron grabbed me by the braid, yanking me away from her. "You're better than this."

I struggled against him instinctively. My scalp felt like it was about to pop off my head; I put my hands to the base of my skull, trying to alleviate the pressure.

"Let me go!" I shrieked.

He didn't. He wrapped his arms around me from behind and held on tight. I flailed and shrieked and . . .

Wait a minute. What was I doing?

I went limp in his arms. Now the only thing I wanted to punch was myself. I wasn't a violent person; this was not like me at all. I'd struck out at Aaron, for god's sake.

"I'm so sorry," I whimpered. "I think it's the nanobots."

All the furious energy melted away, leaving me spent and empty, like a scooped-out melon. Aaron's arms crisscrossed my chest, holding me up.

"What do you need me to do?" he asked.

"Just let go. I'm okay now."

He released me reluctantly, and I took a minute to straighten my coat. Every move was deliberate and controlled. But when I looked up, Elle was right in my face. She shoved me to the ground before I could get out a word of apology. I fell sprawling on the sidewalk, skinning both my elbows. Then she leapt on me, forcing all the air out of my lungs. She was heavier than she looked. Her head was probably full of bricks instead of brains.

"I hate you!" she yelled. "You bitch!"

Aaron attempted to pull her off me, but she was flailing so wildly that it was like trying to put a cat in a bathtub. I'd learned my lesson when Trey had pinned me in the basement. I bucked my hips, hard, and she went flying. Unfortunately, I hadn't planned any further and had no idea what to do next. I could press my advantage, or I could get into the car and lock the doors. While I stood there like an indecisive idiot, she shoved Aaron to the pavement and leapt onto my back.

My chin slammed into the ground, and this time it wasn't cushioned by exercise mats. My vision whited out from the pain. Elle didn't help; she grabbed me by the ears and bashed my head into the concrete. I fumbled at her hands but couldn't get a good grip.

I tasted blood in my mouth, and my eyesight was a blur punctuated by white blossoms of visible pain every time my head hit the ground. I bucked my torso again since it had worked so well the last few times, but all I managed was a millisecond of bash-free bliss.

I heard a far-off roar. My blood pounded in my ears, so at first I thought she might have damaged my hearing, and now all I'd be able to listen to for the rest of my life was a constant "AAAAAAAAAAARGH!"

Suddenly, she was gone.

I struggled to sit up and figure out what the hell was going on, but my eyes wouldn't work. I wiped them with the back of my hands and forced them to focus. My head spun, but at least I was semi-vertical.

Bryan was crouched over Elle's prone body a few feet away. He was howling his hairy head off. His hood had slid back, revealing a fur-covered face. His lips were drawn back from his teeth in a feral smile; he looked ready to tear her windpipe out with his teeth. She covered her face with her hands, as if that would do any good.

As much as I would have liked to see her smeared all over the driveway, I had to do something. I struggled to my feet, and Aaron ran over to me, steadying me until my legs decided to work.

"Elle," I said, pushing him away. "I'll draw him off while you get her into the car."

He looked at me uncertainly. "I can't leave you."

"Go!" I shoved him. "I want her to die, but I don't want her dead. Get what I mean?"

Based on his confused expression, he didn't. But he went anyway.

I jumped up and down and waved my arms. "Hey, Bryan! Over here!"

He stalked in my direction, slow and deliberate and über-scary. I felt like a deer in headlights, only the car was driven by a pack of rabid wolves with black belts. I knew it was the worst thing to do, but I couldn't help it: I ran.

I sprinted around the side of the house, my head whirling. The ground seesawed, and I found myself next to the tree in the middle of the yard without quite knowing how I'd gotten there. But I couldn't stop. I had to get him away from Elle.

Something shifted as my feet pounded through the remains of our unsuccessful vegetable garden. My vision suddenly clicked into place, my gait straightening. I rounded the corner in a blur of movement that felt all too natural. And when I looked back, I saw Bryan, struggling to keep up.

It felt great. I wound through the backyard and up the side of the house, then flew past the car. It felt like my feet were barely touching the ground, but even though I was going so fast, I saw everything in perfect, clear detail. Especially the looks of surprise on Aaron's and Elle's faces. I stuck my tongue out at Elle on my way past, but I don't think she noticed.

The two of them dove into the car, barely managing to pull the doors closed before Bryan hit it. I think he figured he could catch up with me if he went over obstacles instead of around them. His momentum carried him up to the roof, and I waited on the balls of my feet for him to charge again. But he stopped there, crouching on the car, and howled. The guy deserved to be slapped for perpetuating werewolf stereotypes. But before I could whack him a good one, he stopped howling long enough to slam his arm down onto the windshield. It cracked under the pressure.

The urge to attack was irresistible. I was stronger now; I could feel it in the jittery energy that ran down my arms and made my fingers twitch. But I couldn't afford to lose control, not if I wanted to cure us.

And suddenly, just like a switch was flipped in my brain, I knew how. I couldn't believe I hadn't thought of it before: the perfect, portable way to deactivate the bots.

I ran for the house. The sudden movement attracted Bryan's attention; he bounded off the car and loped toward me on all fours. I took the stairs to the second floor three at a time without even breaking a sweat. A low growl echoed down the hallway; I looked behind me before I realized with horror that it *was* me. My belly echoed the sound, the muscles clenching uncomfortably. I was suddenly, horribly ravenous.

The front door exploded into splinters. On his way through the foyer, Bryan crunched the mail bin into kibble. My parents didn't usually mind messes, but something told me they'd mind this.

I made it up the stairs to my bedroom, slammed the door to buy another millisecond, and went for my underwear drawer. The thing I was looking for was all the way at the back.

Jonah had gotten a lot of crap for getting me a high-voltage stun gun at Christmas. He'd said I could use it to protect myself from rogue zombies, and I'd told him he was a complete moron. It was a great holiday season. Full of family bonding.

I picked it up just as Bryan burst through my door, decimating the hinges. The world narrowed to the tunnel of space between us. Time slowed, or at least that was how it felt to me. My arms felt heavy, my fingers clumsy. They tightened on the stun gun, and I almost dropped it.

A red halo framed my vision. My hands went completely

numb. Even my teeth tingled. My skin suddenly seemed too small for my bones. I felt the hair pushing through each individual pore.

It was getting hard to think. I forgot about the weapon I held. I wanted to grab Bryan, bite him, and tear him apart with my hands.

He leapt, rocketing toward me. I clawed his face, but the momentum was too much. I hit my bedroom wall with a sickening crunch. Strangely, it didn't hurt.

Electricity coursed through my body as the stun gun went off in my hands.

CHAPTER
twenty-two

I have no idea how long I lay jerking on the floor after accidentally stunning myself. It certainly wasn't an experience I'd like to repeat. My mouth tasted like I'd been licking the inside of a sewer pipe, and my head felt like I'd gotten a hammer facial, but I still felt pretty lucky.

The reason for my continued existence was pretty obvious: Aaron stood between Bryan and me with a plastic sword in each hand. As I watched, Bryan feinted to the left, trying to get through to the easier prey on the floor. Aaron whacked him, a quick double tap to the shoulder and cheekbone. It probably didn't damage Bryan, but it made him pause. I made fun of Jonah a lot for his pretend swords, but I had to admit they were perfect for fighting off rogue supernaturals.

I struggled to sit up. My brain was having trouble getting my body to cooperate. I'd have to wear gloves the next time I worked on a random attack victim so I didn't contract another case of nanobots. I didn't like how this felt.

Bryan started pacing in front of us, snarling and growling. Neither he nor Aaron had noticed I was awake. I rolled into the scattered bits of dirty laundry under my bed, snatching the stun gun on the way. I didn't want them to see me yet, not before I could stand up without the shakes. My whole body was one big pain receptor set on permanent overdrive. I'd lost track of the ways I'd been smashed and bashed, but there was no stopping now.

Under the mattress I went, through the dust bunnies and a couple of random Skittles, trying not to make a huge racket. Luckily, Bryan and Aaron were fixated on each other and not really paying attention to me. It was a good thing I wasn't, you know, dying.

I reached the vanity in the corner and used it to pull myself to my feet. From here on out, I was all too visible. I'd just have to rush up behind Bryan and hope he was too distracted to notice.

My vision went wonky again the minute I pushed off from the dresser. I staggered the first couple of steps. I didn't think I could do this; my head wouldn't stop spinning. Bryan roared, the sound echoing in the small space. He snatched one of the swords out of the air with a careless flick of his hand. It spiraled right at my face and nearly smacked me on the forehead. I didn't have the time to freak out about that, though.

He'd seen me.

Bryan pounced, knocking me to the ground. I felt pretty grateful, actually, because it was awfully tough to stand.

He tore out a hank of my hair. By this time, my pain receptors were completely overworked; I barely felt it. All I needed to do was reach up and push the button on the stun gun. I almost dropped it twice before I managed to depress the plastic square. Unfortunately, the full-body contact transmitted the shock to me too. My muscles seized, and there was nothing I could do to stop myself from whacking my head on my nightstand. I blacked out for about the millionth time that day.

When I woke up, I expected mass chaos. Instead, I saw Bryan on the floor by my side, Aaron on his cell, screaming, "I'm saying I need a damned ambulance! The address is—" He broke off abruptly, hanging up and rushing to my side the moment my eyes fluttered open.

"Kate," he said. "Thank god. Are you okay?"

"Yeah," I croaked. "Thanks."

I needed help to sit up. Too shaky. But my eyes automatically went to Bryan, looking for the rise and fall of his chest.

He was alive, but totally bald. Like missing-eyebrows bald. If I hadn't been so exhausted, I would have giggled at that.

Aaron helped me up and tried to sit me on the bed. I still had the stun gun; it was practically fused to my palm by now. I gestured with it toward Bryan. I didn't waste my breath on speech; Aaron knew what I needed. He swept me into his arms and carried me over.

I checked Bryan's pulse. Nice and strong. Breath steady. He

even stirred when I poked him. All good things. I sat back with a sense of relief. I could rest for just a moment before I got up and went to find Rocky. She'd be okay. She had to be.

Finally, the whole baldness thing registered, and I groped for my braid in a huge panic. I was so relieved when my hand closed on my hair. I must have stunned myself just in time to avoid complete follicular destruction. And I was pretty sure Bryan's hair would grow back. If not, I could always argue that it's better to be freakishly bald than dead.

But still, I was happy to have my hair. I was enough of a social misfit already without being bald on top of everything else.

"He's going to be okay, right?" Aaron hunkered down next to me, his hand on my elbow to help me balance.

"I think so."

I slapped Bryan's cheek lightly, calling his name. His eyelids fluttered, and then he opened his eyes and grabbed me. I wasn't sure whether he meant to kiss me or beat the crap out of me. I squawked indignantly but couldn't seem to break his grip.

"Do I smell Doritos?" he asked.

I folded my arms so he couldn't see my hands shake, but now I could smell them too, and it was heavenly. So I grabbed the bag next to my laptop and said, "Yeah. You want some? I'm starving too."

We sat among the drifts of hair on my bedroom floor and ate the whole bag while Aaron stood guard.

* * *

Unfortunately, the cheesy goodness couldn't last forever. After the bag was empty, I was still so hungry I could have eaten my own foot. We went into the kitchen, where I polished off an entire loaf of bread, and Bryan ate every slice of cheese in the fridge. Aaron went outside to get Elle, who had been hiding in my car the whole time. I wanted to scoff at that, but I really couldn't blame her. Besides, she was shaken enough to actually be polite to me. I complained that I was thirsty, and she brought me some milk. I drank the whole gallon and immediately felt sloshy-stomached. Maybe that wasn't my best idea ever.

By that time, the dizzy feeling had mostly subsided. Bryan promptly fell asleep on the kitchen tile. Even in his sleep, he looked surprised. Missing eyebrows will do that to you.

He wasn't exactly light, and besides, he seemed pretty comfortable where he was. So I covered him with a striped afghan made with loving care in clashing colors by my aunt Margie, and the three of us retreated into the hallway so we didn't wake him up.

"All right," Elle said. "What do we do now?"

I looked at her skeptically. It seemed like an awfully abrupt about-face to be throttling a girl one minute and offering to help her exterminate some werewolves the next. But she sounded serious.

"Take this." I handed her a slip of paper. "This is Detective Despain's number. Call her once we're gone and tell her everything. She needs to pass the word that the werewolves are vulnerable to stun guns. And keep an eye on Bryan for me." She looked disappointed, but there was no way she'd be able to argue her way out of this one. Someone needed to watch out for Bryan and make sure he didn't go into cardiac arrest or something. "If there's any sign of a relapse, I need to know right away. I don't expect one, though. All we need to do is find Trey, stun him, and feed him some Doritos."

Aaron grinned. "Are they therapeutic Doritos?"

"I was just being nice," I said. "Nicer than he deserves. Will you do it, Elle?"

"Yeah. I guess."

"You're not just trying to screw with me, right? Because Bryan could get seriously messed up if you are."

She threw up her hands. "No! I owe you, okay. For saving me. And for . . . the other thing. I'm sorry, okay?" Then she eyed Bryan skeptically. "Are you sure he's safe?"

"He's safe."

"Okay, then." She started cleaning all the food-related mess off the kitchen table. And I let her.

"So what next?" asked Aaron.

I brought him up to speed in a few sentences, since we didn't have time for all the gory details. He got really pissed-looking when I told him that Trey had stabbed me with a syringe, but I was already moving on. "So," I concluded, "my only problem now is that I don't know how to find Trey. I'd originally planned to hunt him down by smell, but obviously that's not going to happen anymore. And I won't sit around on my duff while he's got Rocky."

"Wait a minute," Aaron said. "You don't mean Trey, do you? Trey Black?"

I nodded. "You bet your sweet bippy I do."

"Trey Black is the murderous werewolf? No way." He shook his head. "He buys all his papers off the Internet. He's not the mad scientist type."

"He's Sebastian's brother. Sebastian is the mad scientist; Trey took the bots from him. He has some delusions of werewolf supremacy."

"Ah." He considered this. "Okay. So why not let the cops handle this? Despain will listen to you."

"Probably, but I'm pretty sure the rest of the cops would think I was batcrap crazy if I sent them werewolf hunting. Trey could kill somebody before they decide to believe us. Or he'll die. The human body just isn't meant to operate at that metabolic level." I swallowed. "I'd rather cure him now and defend my actions later."

Aaron sighed. "So what's the plan, then?"

"Finding him is going to be the hard part. You don't have any idea where he could be hiding, do you?"

"No clue. Why don't I call him?"

I hadn't even thought to try calling him. Apparently, I was one of those genius savants who can calculate square roots in their head but can't function in the real world. It explained a lot.

"Hey, dude," Aaron said. "What's up?" His cell volume was

turned down low, so I couldn't hear Trey's response no matter how hard I strained. "I was thinking maybe we could lift today. You game?" He listened some more, and then his face changed, his lips tightening into an angry line. "All right. I understand. I'll be there." He hung up.

"So?" I prompted.

His voice was ragged. "He wants me to join the pack. Says I can't resist now that he recruited my girlfriend. And if I don't show, he's going to hurt Rocky."

He stood and paced, his hands clenched so tightly into fists that the veins on the back stood out in stark relief against his skin.

"Where is he?" I asked softly.

"School."

At first, I was relieved. It was late on a Friday night, football season was over, and basketball wasn't until tomorrow night. The school would be a nice, empty place to stage our last stand without hurting any innocent bystanders.

And then I remembered. The Rockathon. The auditorium was full of volunteers, and the building would get even busier in an hour when the show choir performed. And they were all doing it because I'd asked them to.

"The Rockathon," I said. "I bet Trey picked it on purpose. He knew it was my thing."

"But how is that possible?" Aaron asked. "Bryan could barely put two words together at the end there, and Trey is perfectly lucid. It doesn't make sense to me."

"Bryan has had some significant strain on his metabolism. All that healing has to consume some major energy, and as far as we know, Trey hasn't sustained that level of damage. And that's why I kept my head as long as I did. If I'd waited any longer, my brain would have melted and dribbled out my ears."

"That would have sucked." He pulled me into a hug, speaking into my hair. "I need a plan, Kate. Tell me what to do so we can catch the bastard."

So I did.

CHAPTER
twenty-three

Aaron and I geared up for battle, and by that I mean we each took a bathroom break and grabbed a pseudosword. I already had the stun gun in my pocket. Just as we started walking toward the front door, it opened. My brother walked in, and I promptly clonked him on the head. I couldn't help it; I was feeling a little trigger-happy.

"Hey!" he yelled, staggering backward and clapping a hand to his scalp.

"Jonah?" I am not usually one for fraternal affection, but I couldn't help myself. I hugged him.

"I'm fine," he said, patting my shoulder awkwardly. "Didn't you read my note?"

"I'm so sorry, Kate," Elle said, walking up behind us. "I took the note off the door and I meant to give it to you, but I was distracted by . . . all the stuff. You know."

"What happened? Are you okay? Where's Despain?" I fired off the questions so fast that there was no way he could answer, but I couldn't make myself stop.

"I regained consciousness just as you were leaving. Other than a headache, I'm fine. And she's at Nanotech Industries trying to find out what the heck they know about this nanobot thing." He paused. "Did I miss any questions?"

"No." I shook my head. "Well, we're en route to kick Trey's ass. You want to come?"

"Heck to the yeah!" Jonah said, sounding geekier than ever. He pumped his fist when he said it too. Lame.

Elle didn't seem to think so, though. She sidled up to him and tossed her hair. "I don't think we've met. I'm Elle."

He nearly piddled. "Um. Hi. I'm Jonah."

"Come back safe, okay?"

She stood on her tiptoes and kissed him on the cheek. I wondered if she'd find him so attractive after she learned that in order to date him, she'd have to change her name to Firestorm and join his harem.

He blushed and muttered something. I had to get out of there before I puked.

"Let's kick some werebutt," I said. It sounded a lot better in my head.

*   *   *

We took Aaron's car back to the school because it was the only one that was undamaged. There was a neon pink Post-it stuck to the dashboard. Elle had that round balloon handwriting that screams, "I'm chipper! I'm perky! I have the IQ of a walnut!" She'd given him her cell number, her home number, and two email addresses. It was totally unsurprising to me that she dotted her I's with hearts. I tore it off the dash, ripped it into little pieces, and threw it out the window. Aaron smiled at me and held my hand the rest of the way there.

The parking lot was overflowing. I was torn between feeling pride that the Epilepsy Foundation would get lots of cash because of an event that I'd established and being afraid that half the student body would get killed in the process. So I started running through our weaponry to distract myself. I had my stun gun. Jonah had a pseudosword, and Aaron had a really cute butt. Not that his butt would be useful in de-botting Trey, but it's always good to have a full catalog of your strengths before going into battle.

"All right, guys," I said quietly. "Jonah, I want you to find Kiki and get her to quietly start pulling people out of the building. Emphasis on quiet, please? We don't want to tip Trey off."

As I expected, he nodded emphatically. Kiki would always be his dream woman, especially since she'd taken him to homecoming. I was pretty sure nothing had happened between them, but pretty sure wasn't all the way sure, and the only thing she would tell me was that my brother was really sweet.

"Aaron, watch my back?" I squeezed his hand and then let go.

"No way." His jaw set in what I was learning to recognize as his stubborn look. "I'm going first."

"But—"

"Please." He got out and stared me down over the hood. "If you won't agree, then we're not letting you go in there at all."

"Yeah," Jonah chimed in. "What he said."

I let out a long, slow breath. "Okay. If that's what you want." But I didn't say what I was thinking, which was that the back entrance wasn't any safer than the front. If Trey had inducted more werewolves into his so-called pack, we might have a problem.

As a precaution, I borrowed Aaron's cell and left Despain a voice mail telling her where we were and what we were doing there. If we disappeared, she'd know what to do.

There was only one set of doors that served the student parking. One of the doors in the middle was propped open. That made me nervous. It was the kind of bottleneck that would make for an ideal attack point. And once again, my grasp of battle tactics surprised me.

Well, I wasn't going to fall into that trap. I pointed toward the open door and shook my head.

"What?" Jonah asked in a too-loud voice.

"Shhhhh!" I hissed. "Try the one on the end."

At least Aaron figured out what I was trying to say. He bypassed the open and inviting door and grabbed the handle of the one farthest to the side. I followed him inside holding the stun gun loosely in one hand. Aaron and Jonah fanned out to either side of me, pseudoswords at the ready.

"I'll go find Kiki," Jonah said.

I nodded, looking down the hall toward the auditorium. A cluster of students stood outside the doors, but I didn't see Kiki. She was probably off somewhere plotting my death because I'd left her high and dry with the Rockathon. Hopefully she'd understand that I'd had to go on a mission of werewolf extermination.

Jonah jogged off down the hallway, his pants practically falling off his skinny hips and pooling on the floor. You'd think he'd wear a belt, but that would make too much sense.

"So where were you supposed to meet him?" I whispered.

"He said he'd sniff me out." Aaron's nose wrinkled. "Which kind of makes me sick."

It was tough to see anything in here; at this end of the school, only the emergency lights were lit, bathing everything in an eerie red glow. The office was to our right, the door cracked open. I took a step inside. Bits of gold crunched under my shoes. There was a case right inside the door that had held a bunch of dusty old trophies from the eighties. The contents of the entire case lay shattered on the floor.

Yep, Trey had been here, all right.

Aaron stood at my shoulder, keeping watch. "Take the stun gun," I said, keeping my voice low. I thrust it into his hands, or tried to, anyway. He wouldn't take it.

"No." He folded his arms. "You keep it. I need to know that you're safe."

"But you're the one he's expecting. As soon as he sees me, he'll know we're on to him. And I'll be a heck of a lot safer if you'd give him a zap as soon as you get close enough. If you make me keep it, then I need to get within striking distance. So you're putting me into more danger, not less."

"And leave you weaponless? Fat chance."

"Give me your pseudosword." After a minute of glowering, he exchanged weapons with me. I smiled reassuringly. "You know how to use the stun gun, right?"

He nodded. I felt kind of funny; I really didn't want to put him in danger. I knew that stereotypically speaking he was supposed to be protective of me and not the other way around, but I'd never done things the way I was supposed to, and I figured it was too late to start now.

"Good." I gave the sword an experimental swing, testing the balance. It felt more comfortable in my hand than I would ever have admitted out loud. I would also never have admitted to practicing with them a little after the whole zombie thing. No way. "Now all we need is a werewolf."

And then, as if on cue, the screaming started.

CHAPTER
twenty-four

Aaron and I ran down the hall toward the auditorium. Everyone else was fleeing in the opposite direction. It was like trying to swim upstream, only the water was full of highly panicked salmon wearing show choir costumes. Everywhere I looked, there were sequined skirts and matching dickies. At least the show choir screamed very musically; I was really tempted to pull out a baton and start conducting.

Within seconds, Aaron and I got separated in the mass of bodies. Someone whacked me in the face; it reminded me uncomfortably of the stampede during the zombie attack. Two people had ended up in the hospital because no one could keep their heads in a crisis.

"Quit panicking, you idiots!" I yelled, raising my sword.

There was a sudden, shocked silence. Everyone froze, their

eyes locked on my pitiful weapon. A howl split the air again, and it took all my willpower not to jump. I needed to appear in control if I wanted them to listen.

"Get outside." I started walking through the crowd, and they parted for me as if by magic. "Get into your cars. Go home. If you see someone without a ride, give them one. Do not leave anyone behind, you got me?" I fixed an underclassman with a glare and he nearly puked on his sparkly cummerbund.

"Yes, ma'am," he said.

"Go," Aaron said, appearing at my shoulder. "Now."

The crowd moved toward the door in a more orderly fashion this time. There was a rising murmur as people began making ride arrangements.

Aaron and I walked toward the auditorium, where Kiki and Jonah stood in front of the closed doors. As we got closer, I could see them shudder and hear the repeated thump of someone beating against the doors from the other side.

I ran up to Kiki. Her hair was mussed, and a pair of bright red scratches ran down one cheek. A trail of blood dribbled down her jaw.

"Kiki, I'm so sorry—" I started, but she cut me off.

"Don't," she said. "I was pretty pissed at you before, but if you were hunting him down, then you were doing the right thing. You were, right?"

The door shuddered, and I heard my name howled from inside the auditorium. "Kaaaaaate! I smell you!"

I swallowed. "Yeah."

"So what now?"

"We're going in."

She opened her mouth to protest, but I pointed at the stun gun in Aaron's hand. Then I shouldered my sword. She looked between the two of us and nodded reluctantly.

"Give me your sweater," she said, beckoning us closer and pitching her voice low. "The scent might convince him you're still out here. I'll put it right up against the door crack and make some noise. Maybe you can take him by surprise."

It was the best plan I'd heard. Okay, so it was the only plan I'd heard, but I still nodded.

"If it gets bad, run, okay?" I handed her my sweater and slipped my coat back on over my Marie Curie tee.

"I will. Now go!" She shoved me down the hallway.

Jonah, Aaron, and I went around to the auditorium's back entrance, creeping in past the dressing rooms and through the backstage. The curtains were half drawn, and a spotlight shone down on a pair of chairs at center stage. One of them rocked lazily back and forth, creaking like the front door of a haunted house.

The lights screwed with my vision; I couldn't see past the edge of the stage at all. And I wasn't going to go out there blind. When I stopped in my tracks, Aaron blundered right into my back.

"Sorry," he whispered.

"Very dexterous," Trey's voice boomed. It sounded like it was coming from the walls, and my head whipped around in a vain attempt to look in every direction at once. The acoustics in here were great for orchestral performances and really crappy for pinpointing the location of a werewolf before he tore your guts out or infected you with killer nanomachines.

"Trey?" Aaron said. "Is that you?"

"Of course it's me, you idiot." A monstrous shadow stretched across the stage. I told myself that it was just a trick of the lights, but when Trey stepped out in front of us and took a seat in one of the rocking chairs, I had to concede that he really had changed. His forehead bulged, and his lips drew back from his gums, exposing fanglike teeth. Even his posture was different now; his shoulders curved forward, thrusting out his neck and making his hands dangle closer to his knees. And of course there was the hair. It even sprouted out of his waistband. I couldn't stop looking at it.

"You brought your girl," Trey said.

"What?" Aaron asked.

"I told you to come alone."

"You didn't really expect me to listen, did you?"

"I will let it slide." He angled his head in a gesture that I think was supposed to be magnanimous. All he needed was a bald cat to pet and a cane topped with a skull and he would have made a great criminal mastermind. "She will be one of my pack mates. And I do mean *mate*. So it's kind of you to bring her to me."

Ew. I really wanted to leave now, but instead I tightened my grip on my weapon. Jonah took a step in front of me, holding his sword high.

"Over my dead body," he said.

"Yummy," Trey replied.

"You need therapy, dude," Aaron said.

"I do not need therapy! I am now . . . a werewolf."

I couldn't help it. I snorted.

"Don't laugh at me!" Trey shouted. "I hate that!" His voice went all growly. If I hadn't known better, I might have thought he was actually a lycanthrope instead of a nanobot-infested tool. I was going to take an inordinate amount of pleasure in watching him get stunned.

Trey launched himself out of the chair, which sailed off the stage and landed with a splintering crash. Aaron didn't even have time to breathe before Trey knocked him to the ground. His hands tightened around Aaron's neck.

Aaron fumbled with the stun gun, his thumb searching for the button. At that range, he would absorb part of the charge too, but he'd be fine. I wasn't worried. He pressed the machine against the side of Trey's neck.

Nothing happened.

He tried again. His face started turning purple, and there was nothing I could do about it. My stupid stun gun was broken or out of charge or something. I really wished I had read the instruction book, although that probably wouldn't have done any good besides maybe making me feel like less of an idiot.

"Tase him already!" Jonah shouted right in my ear, like Aaron hadn't realized he should do something about the fact that he was currently getting throttled.

I couldn't move. My limbs had gone on strike. So I stood there while Jonah let out a battle cry I'd heard a million times before. It was annoying when he did it in the basement, but here in the auditorium from hell, facing down a hairy lunatic, it was impressive. It echoed off the walls and bounced back at us with an almost physical force as he brought a long length of PVC right down on Trey's head.

"AAAAAAAAAAH!" Jonah yelled, raising his arms for another strike.

Trey released Aaron's throat. That was all I had time to see before I backed into the hallway. Not that I was chickening out; I needed to come up with some other way to deactivate those bots. As tempting as it would have been to simply stick Trey's finger into a wall socket somehow, I didn't want to kill him. Not much.

A particularly resounding crash rattled the walls. I half expected to see Trey spring out, covered in the blood of my brother and my boyfriend. But then I heard Jonah's laugh.

"Come on, fiend!" he shouted. "Is that all you've got?"

Clearly, he watched too many movies.

"Flank him, Jonah!" Aaron yelled.

Someone yelped in pain. I couldn't tell who it was. Aaron and Jonah were getting pounded by a werewolf while I stood around like an idiot.

Then inspiration struck.

I dashed to the gym, but the doors were locked tight. My only other choice was to double back and try the locker rooms. I didn't want to think about what would happen if those were locked too and I found myself stuck in a dead-end hallway full of locked doors. But it was the only choice I had, so I snuck down the hall before I could reconsider the wisdom of this course of action.

My sneakers kept squeaking on the tile no matter how carefully I placed them. When I was about twenty feet from the locker room, the fluorescents overhead flickered and then went out. I couldn't suppress a panicked squeak, although I tried. It only took a minute for my eyes to adjust to the dim red glow of the emergency lights, but it felt like an eternity.

"Kaaaate." I heard Trey's mocking singsong before I saw him. He stepped out into the hallway behind me, his hairy face twisted into an expression of gloating satisfaction. He thought he had me trapped. And if these doors were locked, he was right.

I had no idea where Aaron and Jonah were, and the fact that I didn't hear them shouting didn't bode well. If they were conscious, they'd be coming to back me up. No way would I ever believe they bugged out and left me to face Trey alone.

"Come to me, Kate," Trey said, extending a paw.

"I'd rather gargle with battery acid."

I dashed for the door as he let out a snarl of annoyance and gave chase. The door opened under my hand, and I said a silent prayer to the goddess of unlocked locker rooms as I sprinted past the lockers with Trey close on my heels. Thankfully, the showers were empty. Unfortunately, empty doesn't necessarily mean dry. I slipped on the wet tile and went down hard with a hollow popping sound, my leg twisting beneath me. You'd think the pain wouldn't have meant much after all I'd been through, but I was barely holding it together as it was. This was too much; I tried to stand back up and my leg buckled.

Trey slipped on the same wet patch I had and slid straight into the tile wall. His head hit one of the shower nozzles and his body crumpled to the floor. I was torn between leaning over to check on him and continuing to run, but I'd seen enough horror movies to know what happens to the girl when she checks to see if the ravenous killer is still alive. I might not have been the cutesy-young-coed type, but I wasn't chancing it until I was sure those bots had been disengaged.

It was a good choice, because in the two seconds it took me to come to that decision, his eyes flew open. Jonah rounded the corner, and I was so relieved to see him on his feet, even if his face was covered in blood. Aaron was a few steps behind him, and he looked like he'd been through the grinder too.

"Go! Go!" Aaron yelled, meeting my eyes briefly.

He jumped on Trey from behind, locking his arms around his neck. Trey stood up as if the weight was inconsequential, but then Jonah swung at his legs and knocked him back down to the tile.

I hobbled to the door leading to the gym. The machine I needed was hanging right inside the main doors across the room. When I tried to trot toward it, my leg bent sideways. The pain was so intense that I whited out again.

The locker room echoed with howls and thumps, and I

couldn't tell who was winning. But I knew my time was limited regardless; I had to hurry. I dropped to my hands and one knee and dragged myself to the defibrillator. It took me a moment to make my awkward way up to standing and release the case from the wall. If I fumbled this, it could mean my death. I took the box down just as the locker room door flew open.

Trey leapt out, going straight to all fours and loping toward me with his teeth bared. His eyes actually glowed now; he was on the verge of full metabolic overload.

I wobbled. My leg gave way suddenly, and I toppled down on my butt. The defibrillator hit the freshly waxed floor and slid a few feet away.

"Give me a break!" I yelled. "Come on!"

Trey launched himself into the air. Acting on pure instinct, I rolled out of the way. He missed me, but barely. I felt his hair brush against my cheek.

I scrambled for the machine. We'd gotten it when I was a sophomore, and right after they'd installed it, I'd left my gym shoes at home on purpose just so I could read the instructions while everyone else ran laps. So I knew how to work it. I flicked the switch to semiautomatic and pulled out the adhesive pads as Trey scrabbled to his feet, closing the distance between us. His face under all that stupid hair looked pretty surprised when I held out my arms to welcome him.

He hit me with the approximate velocity of a speeding bullet, and we slid across the floor and slammed against the brick wall.

My teeth clacked shut on my tongue so hard that I actually felt the spray of blood hit the inside of my cheek. My knee bent sideways; I shrieked. I wanted to roll around on the floor and clutch it, but I didn't have that luxury.

I smacked an adhesive pad on his arm as his hands closed around my neck. He was breathing hard; I was glad to see him tired because otherwise I think he would have just snapped my bones with his hands like he'd done with Holly and Herbie.

Another pad went on the side of his neck. They were supposed to go on his chest, but this was the best I could do midthrottle. Once the pads were in place, all I needed was to activate the machine. That would have been a lot easier if I could reach it, but my fingers barely skimmed the surface.

His fingers tightened on my throat; his giant teeth snapped shut inches from my nose. My chest burned with the need for air. I tugged on the wires, trying to pull the machine closer, but it refused to budge. Trey growled right in my face. His breath smelled horrible. I didn't want to know what he'd been eating.

The need for oxygen was agonizing, but I concentrated on the defibrillator. I snagged the edge with a fingertip and pulled it closer. My vision started to narrow; I finally found the override button and pushed it.

A high-voltage charge surged through Trey's body. And through mine. By this time, I was an old pro at getting shocked. I came to seconds later. I rolled out from under Trey's twitching body, coughing and holding a hand to my raw throat.

The hair started to shed from Trey's face as I watched, and it was really fascinating until I realized that now he wasn't moving. I dragged myself wearily toward him to check his respiration and pulse. What a pushover I was. I ended up doing CPR on the guy who had just tried to kill me.

Again.

CHAPTER
twenty-five

Aaron dragged himself into the gym just as I was starting CPR. One eye was swollen shut and he was missing a tooth, but his butt still looked great. He called 911 and then took over on the compressions because my knee couldn't support my weight. I sat there and admired the view, which sounds totally skanky but really wasn't. I didn't have the energy to get up. I was impressed that I'd managed to start the CPR at all, because it's hard to balance on one leg and get enough leverage, even for someone as practiced as I was.

That was less my usual egotism and more a statement of fact. In Health and Human Behavior, Mrs. Ludwig had told us most people never need to resuscitate somebody. Apparently, this was true unless you were Kate Grable, in which case you made it a habit of attracting freaks who constantly dropped into unconsciousness. I would have said it was because they were desperate to get close to me, but no one was that crazy except Aaron.

Jonah hobbled into the gym a few minutes later. I couldn't say for sure, but it looked like he'd broken something in his foot, as well as acquired umpteen contusions and a bloody nose. He was using his sword as a crutch. Once he saw that I was okay, he sat down against the far wall and shouted encouragement from there. It was a nice gesture, but awfully distracting. Because I had one more task to complete.

I told Aaron where I was going, and he nodded without breaking count. And then I crawled across the floor and down the hallway. It took forever, but finally I got to the office and found a chair with wheels on it. Now it was much easier; I rolled down the hallway toward the auditorium, where Kiki still crouched in front of the locked doors.

"Kate!" she exclaimed, jumping to her feet. "Are you okay?"

"Have you seen Rocky?" I demanded.

"No. Is your leg broken?" She looked me over with concern on her face.

"Forget my leg. Trey kidnapped Rocky. He must have her stashed around here somewhere."

After a moment of thought, she said, "The box seats. Maybe he locked her in there."

Kiki unlocked the doors and rolled my chair down the aisle. We looked in every one. Rocky wasn't there.

My eyes teared up and immediately covered with a red film. I had blood on my eyelashes. And now my eyeballs. It stung.

"Ow!" I yelled. "Owie ow!" Because I could handle torn ligaments and getting my face bashed in and things like that, but I couldn't handle getting something in my eye.

Kiki crouched at my side. "What's wrong?"

"My eye!" I tried to rub it with my sleeve. "Crap, that hurts!"

Kiki rolled me up the handicap ramp and behind the stage. "There's a sink in the greenroom."

When she shoved me through the door, there was Rocky. She was squirming against the duct tape that secured her to a makeup chair, whipping her head back and forth. The need to get to her was instinctive; I stood up and toppled to the floor with an ungraceful oof.

"Stay there, Kate." Kiki pushed me down by the shoulder. Then she dashed over to Rocky. "I'm so sorry, but this is going to hurt."

Then she ripped the tape off Rocky's mouth. I expected her to scream, but the first words out of her mouth were: "Oh my god, Kate. You look like crap. Are you okay?"

Once the feeling returned to Rocky's hands and legs, she and Kiki lifted me back into my chair and pushed it out to the gym, where Jonah and Aaron were performing CPR. When the EMTs arrived, I had a tough time explaining the drifts of hair scattered around Trey's prone body. Finally, I told them it was like the zombie thing and they left me alone. Despain arrived a couple of minutes later. I sent Aaron out—with a police escort, of course— to get the Nanotech Industries binder.

"I wish you had given me this a couple hours ago," Despain said, tucking it under her arm. "It would have saved me some time. That receptionist is like a pit bull; she kept putting me off."

"Sorry," I said. "I tried."

"That place messed with my cell phone signal," she grumbled. "And you left your house without telling me where you were going. Do I have to leash you the next time we have an emergency?"

"There will be no next time!" I exclaimed, and we nodded simultaneously.

"Sounds good to me."

At first I thought I was going to manage to get away with an order to get my knee X-rayed. All I wanted to do was go home, but I couldn't do that until my parents got back from that B and B. They'd hit the road as soon as Despain called them, but it would still take an hour or so to make the drive. I tried to hide in a corner, but then Aaron told the EMT about the head bashing and everything else, and I ended up strapped to a stretcher wearing a neck brace.

I would have kicked his butt for that, but it was too cute to risk damaging it, and I didn't think my knee could take it anyway. Besides, he leaned over the stretcher and gave me a kiss to make up for it. It felt a little weird with his missing tooth, but it still made my toes tingle.

"The only way I'm going to forgive you for this is if you come along and keep me company," I said.

He grinned. Between the tooth and the black eye, he looked

like a fourth grader. A very cute fourth grader I wanted to share my stretcher with.

"That can be arranged," he said.

"Cool. And Aaron? No more humoring your stalkers. For any reason."

He put his hand over his heart. "Deal."

"Good. Because if I see anyone try to jump in your pants again, I'm going to kill them." He nodded. "And really, death by science geek is a humiliating way to go. I wouldn't want to have to explain that at the pearly gates."

"I wonder how they'd note that on the death certificate."

I laughed, and once I started, I couldn't stop. I was still giggling uncontrollably as they wheeled me into the ambulance and shut the door behind me.

Something told me there was a psych evaluation in my future, but I didn't freaking care. Nothing could be worse than being pounded by a werewolf.

And hopefully, I wasn't tempting fate by thinking that.

The mayor gave me the key to the city. This was rather ironic, because somewhere in the midst of all the chaos, I'd lost Jonah's car keys. We'd had to call a locksmith. Jonah had been giving me crap about it for the past week.

Between that and my appointment with Dr. Dickensheets, I'd had a lot of excitement. Aaron got to help with my MRI; he kept surreptitiously snuggling with me every time the doctor's back was turned. And Dr. Dickensheets wasn't as bad as I'd imagined.

He gave me this cool titanium leg brace and let me help diagnose my knee injury. Torn ACL and meniscus. I had a copy of the MRI and fully intended to hang it on my wall when I got home.

But first I had to get through yet another public appearance without making a total fool of myself. It didn't start out well: I couldn't get out of Jonah's car without assistance. It was not meant for skirts, crutches, or leg braces, let alone all three at once. But he'd insisted on driving me. I think this had less to do with helping me than it did with stopping by to see Elle at her dad's office on the way. They'd gone out on a date on Saturday. The thought of being potentially related to her was enough for me to find religion. I'd gone to church with Mom the next day.

"Would you quit staring and help me?" I huffed, and Jonah finally stopped smirking long enough to help me extract my crutch from the folds of my skirt.

"Here." He offered a hand and launched me to my feet. I nearly went flying into the minivan parked in the spot next to us.

"What the heck?" I demanded.

Jonah curled his arm and made a fist. His bicep actually bulged a little. The shock of it nearly killed me. No way I'd believe that my brother was actually maturing. I'd sooner think he'd been replaced by a pod person.

"Miss Grable! Miss Grable!"

My fraternal reverie was cut short by the herd of reporters that descended upon us. Within moments, I was drowning in a sea of flashing lights and about ready to fake a seizure just to make them stop. The only reason I didn't was because I knew it would end up on the eleven o'clock news.

"Miss Grable, any comment on the murder charges brought against Trey Black?" a woman with helmet head shouted, despite the fact that her mouth was only inches from my ear.

Another reporter chimed in before I could answer. "Do you agree with the decision to shut down Nanotech Industries pending further investigation?"

"Do you intend to go to the memorial service for Hollis and Herbert Langenderfer?"

"Any comments on the rumors that the president intends to award you the Medal of Valor?"

"Do you carry silver bullets with you at all times to protect yourself from further werewolf attacks?"

"You're kidding, right?" I asked. The reporter shrugged sheepishly.

"Do you plan to open a paranormal investigation service?" asked Thornton Cavalier. I remembered him from the last time CNN had interviewed me. He looked more plasticky than ever.

"My plan," I said deliberately, "is to go inside this building and accept the key to the city, and then do some interviews, after which all of you will go away and let me finish my senior year in peace."

"But clearly something is up with Bayview," Cavalier persisted, thrusting his microphone under my chin. "It seems to attract strange phenomena. What do you intend to do if your town is overrun by a genetically engineered Bigfoot? Or visitors from outer space?"

"I'll end it." My words came out a little sharper than I intended. "Bayview is a nice place. And anything that tries to invade it is going to have to come through me first."

"Me too," said Jonah, his voice cracking. He grabbed his pseudosword from the backseat and flanked me as I hobbled through the crowd toward the doors. My parents and Aaron waited at the top. Dr. Burr took my crutches and helped me up the stairs. And Jonah watched my back with his sword in hand.

Somehow, I was less embarrassed by all the attention than I'd expected.

ABOUT THE AUTHOR

Carrie Harris is a geek-of-all-trades and proud of it. She's always been a bit of a brain, so she wrote a zombie book—*Bad Taste in Boys*. And she has hair, so she wrote a werewolf book next—*Bad Hair Day*. Luckily, she won't be running out of body parts anytime soon. Carrie lives in Michigan with her ninja-doctor husband and three monster-obsessed children. Learn more about her at carrieharrisbooks.com.